Liffey Rivers

In the Shadow of the Serpent

Brenna Briggs

ISBN: 1-4392-7138-0
ISBN-13: 9781439271384

Many thanks to Francesca Roberts, Donna Drake, Unateresa Gormley, Terry Williams, Shelly Hathaway and Rachal Barnes

chapter 1

"ONE MUST NEVER wear red on safari, Liffey."

"Never!"

"Even if one's outfit is otherwise suitable, one simply cannot wear red. Red is the color of blood, Liffey, and if one wears red, one is asking for trouble. One might be eaten!"

"O.K.," Liffey replied, somewhat annoyed that her Aunt Jean always used the phrase 'one must' when she meant 'you must' if she was imparting what she considered to be important advice.

"I won't pack anything red."

"One must also never wear white on safari, Liffey. White shows the dirt from dusty roads and ruins the look."

'What look?' Liffey could not believe her aunt was acting like going on safari in South Africa was some kind of fashion event.

"So what color must 'one' wear, Aunt Jean?"

"One must wear khaki, Liffey."

Liffey surveyed the mountain of boxes in front of her and checked them off Aunt Jean's 'Must Bring' list:

Two small flashlights
Waterproof notebook and pen (2)
Sunscreen (2)
Lip balm (4)
Two wide-brimmed hats
Two dust and waterproof handbags
Two duffel bags ? ?
Two small bags for mineral water
Five packages of moist towels
Large aspirin
Snake boots (?) size 8 and size 6B
Sandals: Size 8 and size 6B
Khaki jackets: size medium and size small
Water proof jackets: size medium and size small
Two large camouflage backpacks
Two small camouflage backpacks
Two binoculars
Two camouflage rain hats
Two night goggles
One collapsible snake hook stick
Snake-Away (1)
Four tooth brushes
Tooth paste (2)
Shampoo-Conditioner (2)
Waterproof mascara (2)
Eye drops (1)
Insect bite cream (1)
Hand sanitizer (4)
Blister Medic (1)
Warthog Scent (1)
Insect repellent (2)
Anti-malarial pills (2 bottles)

Ever since Aunt Jean had become an adult Irish dancer and had begun to home school Liffey, if Liffey suggested traveling somewhere where both of them could compete at a feis, she could be fairly certain that her aunt would go for it.

Sometimes Liffey wished she had not asked her aunt if they could go on safari in South Africa for a science unit and then on to a feis in Johannesburg. Aunt Jean thought the safari would make a great chapter in the book she was writing about her unique 'School of Life' teaching methods.

'I don't mind being a guinea pig for Aunt Jean's teaching methods if it means I get to travel to places like South Africa. It's just that she always turns everything into such a major production number.'

"What's in this long box?" Liffey asked.

"You will just have to find out, Liffey. Open it!"

'Is Aunt Jean going to play golf in South Africa on the game reserve?' Liffey opened the long, tubular package which held four blue aluminum snap-together poles.

"What are these poles for, Aunt Jean?"

"They are trekking sticks, Liffey, to use while we trek."

"Do you mean like canes?"

"Yes. One must have the proper equipment while on safari or one might very well pay the consequences."

Liffey could not imagine what the 'consequences' might be for not bringing these canes on safari, but politely asked, "What might the consequences be?"

"Death by snake bite," Aunt Jean replied matter-of-factly.

"O.K., we can hit the snakes with the canes if they try to bite us. Good idea, Aunt Jean."

"What's in this tiny package?"

"It's probably *The Ghost and the Darkness.* I carefully selected this movie, Liffey, for us to practice being terrified in the bush."

"Surely your father has taken you to see the two man-eating lions on display at the Field Museum in Chicago? Those are the same lions starring in this movie."

Liffey was not even going to bother telling Aunt Jean that the two stuffed lions at the museum could *not* be the same lions featured in the movie.

The museum lions were well over a hundred years old.

"O.K.," Liffey said. "A scary lion movie would be good."

"May we please order a pizza while we watch it, Aunt Jean?"

"Certainly, Liffey, we must keep our bodies and minds well nourished during this time of preparation."

❈ ❈ ❈

'I will tell Daddy I went on safari with Aunt Jean *after* we go to the feis in Johannesburg,' Liffey decided, watching her aunt clicking down the hardwood floors in the hallway with her new trekking sticks.

Like 'one' really needed to practice walking with sticks and Daddy would *so* say, "Are you serious?"

"No! You and Aunt Jean are not going to Africa!"

chapter 2

IT HAD BEEN several months since Aunt Jean had moved in with Liffey to home school her while Liffey's father, Robert Rivers, remained in Ireland at his wife Maeve's bedside hoping for signs of improvement.

Every other day, Liffey had the same, almost prerecorded conversation with him: "Your mother is still out of it, Liffey. She has double amnesia and remembers nothing of her previous lives. She has no idea who I am but she is always very cheerful and asks if Liffey is safe. She has fully recovered from the cancer she had ten years ago. Now she must recover from the head injury on the mountain. Your mother is a medical mystery, Liffey."

✳ ✳ ✳

Sam Snyder was sitting in his drafty red 1968 Mustang surrounded by dense shrubbery. He did not mind doing the late watch today because he could experiment with his new monocular night vision goggle equipment.

The lights were turned off inside the Rivers' lake front home and there was a dull television glow leaking through the curtains.

Every few minutes he heard a shriek above the soundtrack of whatever it was they were watching and he adjusted the sound level on his listening device.

Sometimes it was hard to stay awake on night duty. Even with a large thermos filled with coffee. Sam much preferred following Liffey and her eccentric aunt around on the day shift. The aunt was always taking Liffey to shopping malls and other easy-to-watch-from-a-distance places. On the night watch, sitting in his car listening to the Beatles and eating Oreo cookies, he monitored the house and grounds.

Sam wondered if his employer, Attorney Robert Rivers, had told his sister Jean that the Knocknarea gunman's body had never turned up in Ireland. He doubted it from the way she pranced around all day in public with her niece.

❋ ❋ ❋

The mountain rescue team had searched an entire week for the man. The only trace he left behind was a tiny spot of blood a few feet away from the edge of a deep crevice surrounded by tall pine trees. The lab in Dublin said the blood was human.

The Sligo Gardai thought that the gunman had somehow managed to climb out of the ravine and then vanish into the dense pine forest which covered the entire east slope of Knocknarea.

Sam thought this theory was impossible because that man *had* to be dead. He had witnessed what had happened. The gunman's body had been ejected over a cliff by a large black horse like a pebble being fired from a slingshot.

But since he was paid to either sit here drinking coffee all night, or drive around all day following Robert Rivers' strange sister with Liffey in tow, it was all right with him.

'I can't complain,' he thought, popping another Oreo into his mouth. 'This is way more interesting than filling out charts and interviewing embezzlers in Chicago all day. At least I get to see action one in awhile.'

He smiled, remembering being lowered from a helicopter and scaling down the steep cliff to search for the body of the gunman.

'No. That guy is dead. Attorney Rivers is being irrational and overly protective having his daughter watched 24/7 because nobody on earth could have survived a fall like that.'

'Nobody.'

✳ ✳ ✳

Aunt Jean was right. *The Ghost and the Darkness* movie was completely terrifying.

Liffey was hoarse from screaming. It had been a very successful rehearsal for being scared to death in the bush.

If going on safari was going to be anything like having to deal with man-eating lions sneaking into your camp at night and dragging you off, Liffey was not sure she wanted to go to Africa after all.

On the other hand, she knew that her aunt had a way of making you panic about the stupidest things. Like a few weeks ago, after they had read a Sherlock Holmes story called *The Speckled Band*.

Even though the Sherlock Holmes short story had nothing whatsoever to do with Africa, Aunt Jean decided that since it was about a scary snake, it would be a good way to practice being frightened in the bush and would also count as an English home school unit.

After they had finished reading it, Aunt Jean was so unsettled she went all over the house making sure that there were no tiny holes in the walls that a poisonous snake could squeeze through.

No matter that there *were* no poisonous snakes inhabiting the grounds surrounding Liffey's lake house.

No matter that the only wild animals Liffey had ever seen in Wisconsin were squirrels, rabbits, raccoons and an occasional deer.

'Aunt Jean has a way of making you worry about everything.'

Liffey clicked off the television and followed her aunt into the kitchen for a calming down cup of chamomile tea.

chapter 3

NEIL PATRICK ROBERTS ate his Saturday morning Jungle Oats cereal leisurely. Today was not a good day. His arms and back ached from the physical therapy the Sisters made him do every day.

As if his useless legs were ever going to work anyway.

Like he even cared anymore that he was crippled.

He was used to it by now, so why couldn't people just leave him alone? He never bothered anyone. His arms had become strong enough to lift himself in and out of bed and he could easily get himself into his wheelchair each morning.

"Neil, eat your breakfast. You'll be late for therapy," Sister Helen coaxed.

"Yes, Sister, I'm doing my best."

Like being late for therapy was an incentive to hurry.

"And remember, right after PT you have your violin lesson. I hope you have practiced? There are only three weeks left until the Johannesburg Feis."

"I know, Sister. I'll be ready." 'How many times can someone practice The Rakes of Mallow and Saint Patrick's Day?' Neil thought wearily.

"And remember, Neil, you are not competing at this feis. This time you will be the youngest fiddler in South Africa ever to have been chosen to be an official feis musician and you will be paid well to accompany the dancers."

"Yes, Sister," Neil replied, releasing his wheelchair brake and racing out the doorway before Sister Helen could continue her daily lecture.

Today she was lecturing in English. Tomorrow she could be speaking Zulu or German or Afrikaans. Sister Helen was determined Neil would be at the very least, trilingual. The more languages he could master, the better his chances would be to get a good job someday when it was time to leave the home.

Sister Helen was determined he would not be transferred into an adult handicapped facility but would be able to live independently with a good profession.

She smiled at the pale, slim boy hurrying away and shook her head sadly. "How could anyone abandon such a little angel?" she asked the fat tabby cat eyeing the butter on the counter.

"Slow down young man!" she called.

"Yes, Sister."

chapter 4

LIFFEY COULD NOT sleep. Not only could she not stop fixating on the man-eating lions in the movie she had just watched, but Aunt Jean and Max were going at it again.

Their snoring was like listening to an outboard motor boat engine choking and sputtering as it tried to start. The noise Max and her aunt made often kept Liffey awake into the wee hours of the night.

It was only ten days until they were off to South Africa where there would only be one snorer, because Max the Magnificent was staying home with a professional house sitter.

Even though Liffey missed her father and hoped her mother would soon be restored back to normal, she had to admit that living with her Aunt Jean was fun.

'The School of Life' system her aunt had invented was very kid-friendly. It was nothing like Liffey's depressing middle school with its grim-faced teachers and prison classrooms. How many Wisconsin middle school field trips got to go on a real safari in Africa?

Aunt Jean had divided the upcoming safari into two parts. Part one would be at a camp on an elephant reserve. Aunt Jean said that if you ride on an elephant while looking for the Big Five animals, you 'blend in with the environment.'

"It is my duty, Liffey, as your aunt and tutor, to make sure you are not eaten while we track the Big Five. My research has shown me that if one rides an elephant on a game drive, the odor of the elephant masks one's own odor so the big cats and other beasts cannot smell you. Thus, they ignore you."

Part two would be a four-day walk through the bush on foot. Liffey imagined that was why her aunt had purchased the trekking sticks and snake hooks and warthog scent and heaven only knew what else.

Realizing that sleep would not be coming anytime soon, Liffey tiptoed out of her bedroom to find one of the safari guide books Aunt Jean had ordered. She stepped lightly from the dimly lit hall into the darkened living room.

Little pinpricks began racing up and down her spine.

Something was wrong.

Did she hear air escaping from a tire? It was a low, *hissing* kind of noise. Liffey did not have a cat. Neither did her aunt.

A sense of dread began to creep over Liffey like it had a few hours ago watching the man-eater lions pulling people from their tents while they slept.

Another bone chilling *hissssssss* began blowing across the room like the wind starts up right before a heavy rain storm.

It seemed to be coming from the direction of the front door but Liffey could clearly see that the door was shut and had not blown open.

Instinctively, she began to back up slowly towards the hallway door. She inched her way back out into the hall and slammed the door shut just as something thudded on the other side of the door right above her head like a hard-thrown baseball smacking a catcher's mitt.

Liffey's blood felt like ice water. What in the world was *that*?

Should she wake up Aunt Jean? What would she tell her?

She had definitely heard a loud, hissing kind of noise. Then there had been a thud on the other side of the door like something had kicked at it. But it was high above her head.

Maybe a raccoon had made its way into the house through the chimney? But there was a protective screen to prevent animals from getting in that way. And how could a raccoon lunge high up like that? The thud had seemed to come from near the top of the door and as far as Liffey knew, raccoons could not fly.

Liffey recalled someone telling her once that if a raccoon was cornered in your house, it might hiss and then attack you if it had *rabies*!

She had better not put off telling Aunt Jean about this incident until tomorrow morning. She needed to warn her aunt right now. If Max started furiously barking at whatever it was in the living room and Aunt Jean let him out of Liffey's room and into the living room, both of them might have to be treated for rabies if they were bitten. Liffey knew the situation was serious and that she needed to do something about it immediately.

Maybe she could get whatever it was in the living room to go back outside again and not have to wake up Max or her aunt?

It was worth a try.

She went into the kitchen and found the emergency flashlight her father kept inside the pantry on the first shelf. Aunt Jean was just too much of a basket case to wake up and ask for help. Aunt Jean usually made things worse than they already were.

She did not dare risk opening the hallway door to the living room again. The hissing had been totally creepy and very frightening. She would have to go outside and look through the porthole window in the front door.

Maybe shining the bright flashlight into the room would flush out the animal. Then she could open up the front door so whatever it was could run out of the living room while she raced around to the back of the house and let herself back in. That could work. She was a fast sprinter and could easily outrun a raccoon which would at first be blinded by the powerful flashlight.

Quietly, so as not to wake Max, Liffey switched off the house alarm system and crept out through the kitchen door. There was a slight smell of snow in the air. "I should have worn a coat," Liffey groaned, shivering in the chilly night air.

When she reached the outside door to the living room, she realized that she was not tall enough to look in through the thick glass window.

She found a large ceramic planter and managed to drag it over to the window. She stepped up and braced herself against the cold steel door. Then she moved the beam of light through the window back and forth across the room.

At first she saw nothing and had almost decided to give up when something sliced through the stream of light and smashed against the window pane.

Liffey automatically jumped down and away from whatever it was. She was almost certain she had seen fangs scratching the window. Not teeth. Sharp *fangs*!

She sucked in little whiffs of cold night air hoping to give her brain a boost of oxygen so she could think more clearly. Her head felt like it had detached from her neck and floated up above the roof leaving the rest of her body spread out all over the front lawn.

Had she seen a *snake* in her living room?

Something with a large, flattened, hooded head like a cobra with huge fangs?

Liffey forced herself to remain calm.

Whatever was in there, she knew she was safe on this side of the door but she had to get back into the house and warn Aunt Jean not to go into the living room.

What if Max started barking and Aunt Jean let him into the room before she made it to the back door? Her aunt might think there was a mouse in the house and open the door for Max to patrol.

The man-eating lions' movie seemed like Bambi compared to what Liffey had just witnessed. How could there be a *snake* baring its ugly fangs at her through her own front door window? Huge cobras did not exactly live in Wisconsin living rooms.

Liffey felt off-balance. Her brain was wiggling like the dancing cobras she had seen in old movies swaying back and forth to flute music being played by men with beards wearing turbans wrapped around their heads.

Robert Rivers had told Liffey that the cobras were deaf and moved to the vibrations, not to the music.

Anyway, what did that matter now?

Who *cared* whether cobras did or did not live in Wisconsin and whether they were or were not deaf?

What was one of them doing in her living room? Apparently, she had barely missed being fanged a few seconds ago when she slammed the door shut on the thudding hisser.

Liffey began to tremble in the cold night air. Sometimes the realization that her life often seemed to be only seconds away from total disaster was just too much to think about.

One freaky thing after another.

It was good that she had been practicing being terrified earlier tonight because she was *way* beyond terrified now.

She must have twisted her ankle a bit when she jumped down from the ceramic planter because it throbbed painfully as she hurriedly limped to the back of the house and let herself in.

Max and Aunt Jean were still snoring away.

Liffey dialed 911.

If this was not an emergency, nothing was.

chapter 5

SAM WAS WRENCHED from his night watch drowsiness by a beam of light aimed at the Rivers' house. He immediately adjusted his night vision equipment and Liffey Rivers came into focus.

She was standing on an urn looking into her front door window, holding a flashlight. Before he could sharpen her image, she jumped down and limped away towards the back of the house.

'That kid never sleeps,' he thought. 'It's a good thing she is still years away from her first driver's license. She'd probably think nothing of driving to Chicago at midnight for a slice of Uno's pizza.'

He settled back into his seat and reached for his tenth Oreo cookie, trying to decide if he should follow Liffey to the rear of the house to make sure she got back in safely. He had heard some static noise from the living room and then what sounded like a door slamming shut before Liffey had come around to the front of the house with her flashlight.

Before he could make up his mind whether he should check on Liffey, the sound of approaching sirens cut through the silence and there were flashing red and blue lights in his rear view mirror.

He jumped out of the car. 'Did I miss something? Was someone hurt in there?'

Because he did not wish to reveal his presence to the police, he stood motionless in the evergreen bushes, watching the scene unfold across the street.

A police squad car turned into the driveway. Two officers jumped out and walked directly to the front door of the house.

Instead of knocking on the door, one of them stood up on the urn which Sam had seen Liffey jump off just a moment ago. The officer looked through the front door window with a high powered flashlight and then jumped down like he had seen a ghost.

Another squad car arrived with two more officers. They stood in a group conferring and Sam could see that their body language was tense. Almost like this was some kind of hostage situation.

'What in the world was going on inside that house? What had the officer seen through the porthole door window? Liffey must have called the police right after she had jumped off the urn and limped to the back of the house. What or who was in there?'

He switched on his police scanner and turned up the volume of his house listening surveillance equipment.

❄ ❄ ❄

Aunt Jean had her hand on the living room door knob and was beginning to twist it open when Liffey entered the hallway from the kitchen to stand guard until the police arrived.

"NO! STOP! You can't go in there, Aunt Jean!" Liffey shrieked as she ran to the door and body blocked it.

"Liffey, what's going on here? Why are there flashing lights and sirens outside? Are you sick? Has something happened?" Before Liffey could answer, four bewildered police officers entered the house through the kitchen door.

"Lady, there is one *huge* snake in your living room that looks like some kind of cobra! We called animal control in Milwaukee and they are looking for a herpetologist to ID it so we will know what we are dealing with here."

Aunt Jean looked puzzled and disoriented. She turned to the police officers and said, "I beg your pardon? What do you mean there is a *cobra* in my living room? Are you completely mad? Cobras do not live in Wisconsin. You must be mistaken."

Aunt Jean put her hands on Liffey's shoulders and tried to move her away from the living room door so she could go in to investigate but Liffey stood firm. "I don't understand. We are not on safari yet. This makes no sense."

"I could not agree with you more, lady," said one of the policemen firmly taking hold of her elbow. He escorted her away from the door into the large, cheerful kitchen. Another officer immediately replaced Liffey and positioned herself in front of the living room door.

"Here, let's get you into a chair," said a third officer, taking charge of the situation and gently guiding Aunt Jean, who looked like she was ready to faint, to the kitchen table.

"Liffey, is it? Could you please make some coffee for your mother?" Liffey did not bother to correct the officer.

✳ ✳ ✳

The police scanner revealed that a 911 poisonous snake call had come in from the Robert Rivers' residence on Lake Shore Drive and that two squad cars had been dispatched. Sam could tell from the conversation he was eavesdropping on in the kitchen that the police were worried.

Sam was positive no one had come towards the house from the front where he was stationed, but there was a large lake in back of the house to consider.

Even though the piers and boat slips had been taken down for the winter, the lake had not yet frozen over. A boat carrying a deadly snake could have been launched from several places along the shoreline. Paddling a boat over to the Rivers' estate would be easy.

Anyone who might have been at the Rivers' house at one time or another would probably know that the kitchen door contained an electronic dog door at its base. 'Or in this case, possibly a 'snake deposit' door,' Sam thought. Still, none of the security or surveillance systems had indicated there was anything unusual happening on the grounds.

It did not matter *how* it had happened. It *had* happened, and now he would have to explain to Robert Rivers that he had apparently let his guard down and allowed a cobra to enter the Rivers' home putting his boss's daughter and sister in mortal danger.

✳ ✳ ✳

Dr. Harry Carmichael, a retired herpetologist from Chicago, had been searching in the dark with a high-powered flashlight for the past ten minutes when he saw the pulsing red and blue lights in the driveway about a block away.

'Oh dear, someone must have spotted my Hannah. I hope she didn't bite that little white dog and try to swallow it. She has no judgment anymore about what she eats.'

He tightened his grip on the snare poles he would use to control his escaped King Cobra and walked quickly towards the

Rivers' residence. He pulled a wagon behind him carrying a large trap box containing a foot long garter snake for bait.

Hannah liked late night snake snacks.

He hoped he would not be in trouble with the police for allowing his Hannah to escape.

If the police asked him about the garter snake snack, he would assure them that it was *not* a protected Wisconsin Butler's Garter Snake, just a garden variety garter snake. He kept a supply of them in his basement for Hannah.

Dr. Carmichael thought it was important for his Hannah to enjoy an afternoon sunbathing session in the solarium each day and a quick slink around the enclosed back yard rock garden every night for some fresh air.

Even though the chilly night air made Hannah lethargic and it was too cold for cobras to survive for long outside this time of year in Wisconsin, he had let her out into the gated rock garden in the backyard which was surrounded by high stone walls with barbed wire at the top to prevent snake escapes.

He could smell snow in the air. Soon these outside sessions would not be possible.

Somehow, Hannah had escaped when he had gone back inside his cottage to make a cup of hot chocolate.

Dr. Carmichael had a license to keep Hannah as well as a fine reputation as an emeritus herpetologist in the Zoology Department at the University of Chicago where he had specialized in cobras in captivity.

Dr. Carmichael did not know how Hannah had managed to get over the twenty-foot-high garden wall and through the wire barrier.

Unless he had forgotten to close the garden gate again.

chapter 6

BLACK MAMBA WAS sleeping in a large trap box inside a large cage.

The Cape Town herper opened the plexiglass sliding door and carefully lifted the trap box out of the cage and into a wooden shipping crate for the long trip to Johannesburg.

The herper had been extremely cautious.

Black Mamba did not get the nickname 'Slender Death' because it was harmless. This one was fourteen feet long and could strike a lethal blow from as far away as five feet.

Selling a snake as deadly as Dendroaspis Polylepis normally involved a lot of paperwork and permits. The herper was nervous and a bit ashamed that he had complied with the instructions from the mamba's anonymous buyer not to register this sale.

What he had done was clearly dishonest, but the padded envelope stuffed with diamonds had stunned him and turned his conscience into mush. He was a rich man now.

He hoped the buyer of this snake knew how to handle it. One bite from Black Mamba contained enough neurotoxin and cardiotoxin to kill twenty-five grown men.

✳ ✳ ✳

Another black mamba in South Africa slithered out from a small hole at the bottom of an abandoned termite mound where it had lived peacefully for five years. Twenty-eight hours ago the snake had collapsed its inky black mouth and swallowed a large brown rat. The rat had been completely digested and it was time to hunt again.

The black mamba glided along through the tall savanna grasses effortlessly, tongue flicking, head raised four feet off the ground, searching for prey.

✳ ✳ ✳

Liffey Rivers finished skimming a National Geographic Magazine article about leopards in South Africa.

The police had left.

The totally bizarre neighbor with the snake box had captured his horrifying cobra and gone home.

Liffey shuddered. She did not yet have the courage to go back into the living room to look for the safari guide so she went into her father's extensive library to search for a boring Irish history book to help her fall asleep.

Liffey dreaded her father's Irish history lectures and ordinarily did not want to read any of his dull books, but tonight she was desperate. She needed more than her lava lamps to help her fall asleep.

She found a small brown leather missal on one of the book shelves. It was a copy of a book written by an ancient monk from Belgium named Jocelyn and in the book there was an entire chapter about Saint Patrick kicking all the snakes out of Ireland.

This was, as her lawyer-father would say, 'directly on point.' One particular passage jumped out at Liffey:

'Indeed it has come to our knowledge that when certain persons had been bitten by serpents, the scrapings of the leaves of books brought out of Ireland were put into water and given them to drink, which immediately expelled the spreading poison and cured the swelling.'

If there were going to be poisonous snakes striking at her in the bush, she needed more protection than Aunt Jean's trekking sticks and waiting around for antivenom to save her life after she had been bitten.

Liffey had researched the snakes which inhabited the game reserve areas where she and Aunt Jean were going to be trekking and had learned that a single bite from a black mamba snake could kill someone in less than thirty minutes.

And there were other snakes. Adders and vipers that could drop out of trees on your head and sink their long fangs into your neck before you even saw them coming at you.

It was apparent to Liffey that she had to take every precaution she could think of not only to avoid snake bites in the bush, but also to manage the situation if the worst happened. Maybe the ancient remedy Jocelyn the monk described could actually help in a snake bite emergency.

Liffey had not purchased any holy books in Ireland but she did buy a copy of *Harry Potter and the Prisoner of Azkaban* in Sligo because she wanted the UK book cover.

The words in her father's old monk book said that if scrapings from *any book brought out of Ireland* were placed into water and drunk by the person who had been bitten, Saint Patrick's ancient blessing would expel the snake poison or at least stop it from spreading.

Liffey considered how very Hogwortish this all sounded. 'It can't hurt though. I will use Daddy's paper shredder and shred the Harry Potter title page and then put the paper particles in a baggie. I will put some of it in my canteen when we go trekking in the bush.'

It had been a long, crazy night and it was totally time to sleep. She turned on her three lava lamps and prepared to stare herself into oblivion.

If only she could stop thinking about the hooded head of the cobra gaping at her through the window and the man-eating lions of Tsavo.

She had to remember to pack her emergency spaghetti and meatballs.

Just in case it would be hard to find them in South Africa the night before the Johannesburg Feis.

chapter 7

AUNT JEAN WOKE up from a troubled sleep.

There had been a cobra in her house last night and police officers and a man who called himself a 'herper' who said ridiculous things like, "You can keep a cobra, but you can never own one."

Liffey had almost been bitten by that man's monstrous snake. Dr. Herper said that the venom glands in his snake had been removed and it was completely harmless, although it might have tried to have a go at little Max if the opportunity had presented itself because his snake was getting old and seemed to have forgotten how to 'size up' its meals.

"Poor Hannah can't tell the difference anymore between a mouse and a small dog," Mr. Herper had told her.

Aunt Jean had almost choked thinking about that creature of the night trying to swallow Max the Magnificent.

Aunt Jean had agreed with Dr. Herper, or whatever his name was, that 'Hannah' might not be deadly poisonous, but how would *he* like to have that snake's hideous fangs piercing through *his* skin like sharp nails?"

'That man needs to have his head examined for letting that revolting monster out into his backyard like some kind of normal pet.'

Dr. Herper told Aunt Jean that cobras were considered sacred in some places and there was a cobra god called Wadjet which protected the pharaohs. Aunt Jean shuddered.

Wherever the pharaohs were these days, they could keep their loathsome cobras to themselves.

✳ ✳ ✳

The clock said 9:00 a.m. It was time to work on Liffey's big surprise.

Aunt Jean went over the Big Five list again in her head, determined that each of them would be represented on the spectacular new solo dress she was designing for Liffey to wear at the feis in Johannesburg:

Elephant

Rhino

Lion

Leopard

Cape Buffalo.

She was somewhat disheartened that the Big Five beasts Liffey and she had been studying for the past three weeks were so colorless and drab.

'How can one create a colorful solo dress with faux elephant skin, mud-colored cape buffalo and gray rhinoceros hides?'

'Why can't the giraffe and cheetah replace the dreary rhino and cape buffalo on the Big Five list?'

"Dull grays and dirty browns? I think not," Aunt Jean told Max the Magnificent who was busy chewing a sock under her sewing machine.

"Faux leopard would definitely work. Possibly for the cape. And the mane of a lion might make an interesting solo dress crown or fringe trim. But I simply cannot create beauty from faux rhino, elephant and cape buffalo hides."

She sighed. It was not easy being a brilliant Irish dance dress designer.

Doctor Bernard Morrow was sorry he could not give the American attorney better news about his wife's condition, both physically and mentally.

It was hard for him to believe that Mrs. Rivers' aggressive cancer was in remission. Especially if what her husband said was true, that she may have been taken off a plane and left for dead somewhere on the west coast of Africa.

It did not make medical sense.

He had studied Maeve Rivers' files from the States and her prognosis had been very poor ten years ago. Yet this woman's vital signs were now excellent.

The serious blow to her head up on Knocknarea had not caused any apparent brain damage and except for the amnesia that still clung on, he told Robert Rivers his wife was fit to go home.

He urged Attorney Rivers to seek further medical evaluation in the States. "I need to run a few more tests and it will take me at least a week to reserve a medical evacuation plane. I am sorry you and your wife will have to spend Christmas here in Sligo, Attorney Rivers."

Dr. Morrow said he had no idea what Robert Rivers might expect as to his wife's memory returning. He thought that eventually she would not spend so much time sleeping and perhaps some or even all of her memory might come back.

✳ ✳ ✳

Maeve Rivers' eyelids were fluttering open when her husband returned to the small hospital room. Standing by her bed was Liffey's good friend, Sinead McGowan.

She handed Mr. Rivers the small voice recorder she had switched on when Maeve had begun to talk in her sleep.

"Thanks, Sinead."

"No bother, Mr. Rivers. You know how much I enjoy coming here and talking to Mrs. Rivers about Liffey and I know she listens sometimes. I can tell. At the moment though, she seems to be having a bit of a bad dream."

Sinead was right, this dream was a nightmare.

Maeve was tossing around in her bed like a boat caught up in a bad storm. She stopped thrashing and became very still when Robert Rivers began to tuck her back in under the blankets.

Before he could stop her, Maeve unexpectedly grabbed the bedrail and pulled herself down to the cold linoleum floor where she sat hugging herself like a frightened child.

When Robert Rivers and Sinead tried to help her up off the floor she resisted and spoke in a haunted, trancelike voice:

"NO!! Liffey go home! *Go home*! Mahmbah! No feis…tall grass…no Africa. Go home, Liffey! Blak Snek Mahmbah!"

Sinead gave Robert Rivers a quizzical, concerned look.

He shook his head sadly.

"From several things Maeve has said recently, my staff investigators in Chicago think she may have been left in a jungle on the west coast of Africa en route to Switzerland for treatment."

Sinead nodded and quietly tiptoed towards the door, stumbling a bit and fumbling with the doorknob on her way out.

"See you tomorrow then, Mr. Rivers."

❊ ❊ ❊

"I'm taking you home soon," Robert Rivers said cheerfully as he helped his wife back up to her feet.

"Please don't worry about our little girl, Maeve."

"Liffey is safe with her Aunt Jean in Wisconsin."

chapter 8

THE COMFORTABLE SOUTH African Airways plane was somewhere over the Atlantic Ocean when Aunt Jean announced that she had decided to master the isiZulu language during the long flight to Johannesburg.

Liffey pointed out that you could not 'master' any language, let alone one as difficult as Zulu, on a twenty-four hour flight.

Aunt Jean said her nerves were frayed and learning isiZulu would distract her. She had almost fainted after she charged the round-trip airfare for their trip to South Africa and later discovered how much money she had spent.

Liffey had tried to reassure her that 50,000 South African Rand was way less than 50,000 U.S. dollars but Aunt Jean did not seem to understand. Liffey checked the currency exchange online and discovered that her aunt had charged over 6,000 U.S. dollars for their round-trip airfare.

It occurred to Liffey for the first time that they must be a very wealthy family to be able to afford this kind of traveling. 'If we are *not* rich, then Aunt Jean will be in major trouble if Daddy finds out.'

Liffey hated how her aunt had started calling Johannesburg, 'Jo'burg,' like she was some kind of regular traveler to South Africa.

Like she could even find it on a map.

❊ ❊ ❊

Liffey doubted she was prepared for this feis.

Practicing with Aunt Jean over the past few weeks had been very difficult after her aunt had read an article about Fen Shui decorating in a magazine.

The article said it was important to get rid of all the clutter in your life and that if you did not, it could ruin your creativity.

Since Aunt Jean had wanted a dance studio in their home anyway, she removed all of the furniture in the pine wood dining room and had it put into storage to create a positive energy flow.

"If your father objects when he returns we can always un-Fen Shui the room, Liffey."

There was no doubt in Liffey's mind that her father *would* object when he saw his empty dining room with nothing in it except a long metal bar attached to the wall for stretching exercises.

Dance practices with Aunt Jean had been either eight hours a day or no hours a day.

On the eight hour days, Aunt Jean said things like: "Dancers in South Africa learned how to leap over poisonous snakes before they could even walk, Liffey. We must practice our leapovers and make ourselves hold them just a little bit longer each time."

Liffey was required to critique her aunt's steps and had to be careful that she did not accidentally slip and criticize her aunt's sloppy technique because Aunt Jean did not want to hear the truth.

At the end of these eight hour days, Liffey was too mentally exhausted from constantly praising her aunt to work on her own steps.

On the zero practice hour days, Aunt Jean would say things like: "Liffey darling, it is beyond me why we Irish dancers have to endure so many classes and endless practices when it is all so very simple. Just point your toes at every given opportunity and everything else will fall right into place."

Liffey had missed the entire last month of Irish dance classes because Aunt Jean had developed a bad habit when she drove her car of pointing her right foot each time she switched it from the accelerator pedal to the brake.

This caused the car to jerk a lot because her toe-pointing-foot often could not make it to the brake pedal fast enough to avoid hitting the car in front of her unless she braked hard.

Because of this erratic driving, Aunt Jean had been stopped several times by the local police who were suspicious of her lurching and did not want to hear about her toe-pointing theory.

Even worse than the frequent cop stops, Liffey had begun to get motion sickness when she rode in the car with her aunt. So she chose not to remind Aunt Jean about the weekly ninety-mile-round-trip drive to her Irish dancing classes and Aunt Jean never brought the subject up.

❋ ❋ ❋

'I am so not going to place at the Johannesburg Feis,' Liffey thought glumly, putting on her earphones to block out any Zulu words her aunt might want to share with her.

She flattened her seat into a comfortable sleeping position, snuggled into her soft duvet and stole a glance over at Aunt Jean who had evidently forgotten all about becoming a Zulu language expert.

Aunt Jean had put her books down and was watching an in-flight movie while she sipped a glass of white South African wine and nibbled on something that looked like beef jerky called 'Biltong.'

Liffey yawned. It was time to go over Aunt Jean's Big Five drill for the last time:

Lion

Leopard

Elephant

Cape Buffalo

Rhino

By tomorrow afternoon, they would be living in the wild, roughing it up on safari at an elephant reserve.

Liffey seriously doubted that her Aunt Jean could take a real safari. She got upset about things like breaking a fingernail and now she was suffering from a 'Post-Traumatic Bling Disorder' according to the doctor at the Liberty Torch Feis in New York.

Liffey knew it had been a really bad idea to cram a feis in on the day before they left on safari but Aunt Jean wanted one last live practice before she danced in South Africa.

There had been 1,600 dancers at the feis in New York and thousands of Swarovski crystal-smothered solo dresses and rhinestones on poodle socks and other sparkling stressors which finally put Aunt Jean over the edge and she had collapsed.

But that was yesterday. Maybe they would see one of the Big Five tomorrow before the next sunset.

One thing Liffey knew for certain was that she never wanted to see another snake again as long as she lived.

❊ ❊ ❊

Sam Snyder followed Liffey Rivers and her aunt to the 'Passengers Only' entrance inside the General Mitchell International Airport terminal in Milwaukee. He had notified Attorney Rivers that his daughter and sister had made plans to go to an Irish dance competition in New York. They were to return Sunday night and he would be waiting. He would follow the shuttle to long term parking where Jean had parked her pink Cadillac and then follow them home to the house on the lake.

In the meantime, the Rivers home would be occupied by a professional house sitter and under constant surveillance.

Sam had made arrangements for Liffey and Jean to be tailed by the Martin Detective Agency while they were at the feis in New York.

※ ※ ※

Bob Martin followed the airport limo the Rivers ladies had boarded in front of their hotel after the Irish dance competition had ended.

When the limo reached the airport, Detective Martin decided there was no good reason for him to follow them all the way to their airline terminal. It had already been a long, uneventful two days hanging around in the hotel lobby making sure they did not leave the hotel unaccompanied.

Nothing would happen to them in the airport. There were security guards everywhere.

A few hours later, Sam Snyder called the Martin Agency in New York and said that the Rivers ladies had not arrived as expected at the Milwaukee airport on their return flight.

Bob Martin did not tell Mr. Snyder that he had not followed the ladies into the airport.

When Sam called the airline to see if they had checked in, he was told they had been 'no shows.'

They had disappeared.

chapter 9

NEIL HAD APPEARED on the altar in the private chapel of the Sisters of the Holy Childhood nine years ago. His thin little legs dangled motionlessly from an expensive high back baby stroller. He was wearing a light blue sailor suit with a matching hat and white leather sandals.

He looked like a little angel. Next to him was a small suitcase. In the suitcase there was a teddy bear, a quilted baby blanket, snap-on pajamas, and a change of diaper.

Next to the small suitcase was a very large athletic bag stuffed with five billion South African Rand in 200 Rand denomination banknotes.

No note. No instructions.

Just a large fortune.

Sister Agnes had found the little boy when she brought fresh flowers to place on the altar. At first, the Sisters discussed among themselves whether or not they should contact the authorities. There had been many conflicting opinions.

Sister Helen said, "No, we will keep him. We will build him a lovely room in the new wing we will construct using the miraculous money he brought to us. We have been desperate for funds to build the new addition. We have fifteen children sleeping in the halls as it is. God has sent this money to us to provide for this child and many others."

"Pardon me, Helen, but I don't think *heaven* has sent us an athletic bag full of cash. It could very easily be drug money or heaven only knows what else. We must contact the authorities and…"

Sister Helen interrupted Sister Agnes.

"Do you think for one minute, Agnes, that this suitcase full of money is not at risk if it goes anywhere other than right into our own hands where it has already been deposited? Some corrupt official will buy a yacht and then build a palace with it if we don't use it for the good of our children."

Sisters Anna, Loyola, Patricia, Mary, Joan and Catherine all agreed with Sister Helen.

Eventually it was unanimous. The Sisters would follow the news carefully every night, listening for a 'missing child' story. If a child had been reported missing, they would immediately contact the authorities.

In the meantime, a twenty-bed new addition was added on to the Holy Infant Home for Disabled Children along with a small indoor pool for physical therapy and a new nursery for abandoned newborns.

The Sisters had named their little altar angel, 'Neil Patrick Roberts.' It was a name that would blend in with the other students at the secondary school he would someday attend funded by the education trust fund they had established for him.

There was also a medical trust fund set up for baby Neil because Sister Helen 'felt it in her bones' that there would be a breakthrough someday and Neil's floppy little legs would be miraculously restored.

chapter 10

AUNT JEAN WAS examining the amenity kit the airline had provided when Liffey awoke from a sound, dreamless sleep. "I can't wait to tell Daddy how these seats turned into cradle beds, Aunt Jean! He always books us in coach."

"No, Liffey. We cannot mention this School of Life field trip to your father. He simply would not understand, Liffey, darling. If he ever finds out, I will get a two day lecture about spending money irresponsibly. I am glad you woke up. We will be landing soon at the Oliver Tambo International Airport."

"Oliver Tambo was one of the founding fathers of South Africa, Liffey."

Liffey waited for her aunt to continue but she had apparently already finished her Oliver Tambo history lecture.

'Why can't Daddy's history lectures be that short? He would have read ten books about South Africa before this trip and then talked about Oliver Tambo and Nelson Mandela all the way to Johannesburg.' It was obvious Aunt Jean had only read a few sentences about Oliver Tambo in the South African Tourism brochure she had found tucked into the seat pocket in front of her.

She must have missed the Nelson Mandela story.

Liffey did not let on that she had read the same brochures last night.

"That should count as our history unit for the day, Aunt Jean. I will remember the name Oliver Tambo."

Aunt Jean nodded and recorded one history unit in the small School of Life Records notebook she carried with her.

✳ ✳ ✳

Liffey hoped the plane might fly low enough for her to spot a large elephant or giraffe before they landed. According to Aunt Jean, they would land only a few hours away from the elephant reserve where their safari would begin.

"Now Liffey, dear, we must remember we will be in a foreign country soon and things will not be the same in South Africa as they are in Wisconsin." Liffey suspected this might be the first time Aunt Jean had thought about this.

"We must be brave and pretend that we know what is going on even if we do not."

"Wouldn't it be better to ask questions if we don't know what is going on, Aunt Jean?"

"No, Liffey. It would certainly not be better. Asking questions is a sign of weakness. We must give the impression that we have been on safari many times so the animals in the wild do not take advantage of us."

Liffey had no idea how to reply to this bizarre proclamation by Aunt Jean. "O.K., Aunt Jean. I won't ask the wild animals any questions."

"Thank you. I knew you would understand, Liffey."

There was no doubt about it. Liffey was about to go on safari in Africa with an insane person.

✳ ✳ ✳

Oliver Tambo International Airport was huge. Aunt Jean collected their luggage and arranged to have their Irish dance dress carriers shipped to the hotel in Johannesburg where they would be staying after the safari.

A scary thought entered Liffey's mind walking through the airport arrivals area. Had Aunt Jean remembered to look into how they would be traveling to the elephant reserve?

"Are we renting a car, Aunt Jean? You know they drive on the left here, like in Ireland."

"No, Liffey. I have made other arrangements," Aunt Jean said.

She was about to explain when Liffey spotted a uniformed chauffeur standing by the exit door holding a handwritten sign that said: 'RIVERS FAMILY.' Liffey was horrified.

"Aunt Jean! Are we going to be driven to the elephant reserve in a limo?" She had expected that her aunt might hire a driver but she had imagined it would be a ranger driving a jeep, not a uniformed, black capped chauffeur driving a limousine.

"We will be exposed to the elements soon enough, Liffey, darling. This will be our last taste of civilization before we abandon ourselves completely to the bush."

"South African pizza is waiting for us in the limo."

Liffey had to admit that pizza sounded good but a formal driver and a limo was *not* the way she had imagined starting off on safari.

'Oh well, at least when we get to camp, Aunt Jean's extravagant lifestyle will be put on hold. I hope she has some coping skills.'

✳ ✳ ✳

The black mamba sunned itself on a large flat rock next to the abandoned insect mound. Yesterday's menu of three mice had been completely digested and it was time to eat again.

Soaking up solar energy from the sun gave the mamba sufficient energy to move through the tall grass at twelve miles per hour.

Fast enough to wear down most of the small animals it would stalk today.

✳ ✳ ✳

Black Mamba arrived in Johannesburg in a dirty red van inside a trap box secured in a sturdy wooden crate.

The driver's instructions were to ring the bell, deposit the box on the doorstep and leave immediately without getting a signature from the recipient.

The ride had been bumpy and stressful for Black Mamba.

It was hungry and thirsty after the long, hot journey from Cape Town.

✳ ✳ ✳

When the handsome young man watching from the window on the second floor saw the red delivery van leave, he exited the abandoned warehouse through the back door and moved the Mercedes truck parked in back of the building around to the front. He carefully lifted the wooden crate into the empty truck.

He was tempted to take a look at the snake but did not.

His instructions were to park the truck in a nearby car park under the Toyota Motors sign where the snake would be picked up by a local herpetologist.

There was a blue Ford rental car waiting for him under the same Toyota Motors sign. He was told to drive it to his hotel and wait for further instructions.

chapter 11

EVEN THOUGH LIFFEY was sitting in a limo eating vegetarian pizza and watching an elephant video, she could easily picture already being on safari.

She was standing on a high wooden platform watching far-away herds of zebra grazing in a sea of tall grasses.

Her cot was covered with mosquito netting in the small tent she and Aunt Jean shared.

There were late night campfires under fields of brightly shining stars burning above in the coal black sky.

In the distance, Liffey could hear the roar of a lion and the snarl of a leopard...

As the air conditioned limo drove northeast, out of the spaces inhabited by humans, towards a scruffy, ancient world where animals still made most of the rules, Liffey could tell that Aunt Jean was nervous and preoccupied. She was looking at a map and saying things to herself like, "I did not realize camp would be so far from Jo'berg."

Liffey cringed. It could be worse. At least she had not started calling Johannesburg, 'Jozi,' another nickname for the largest city in South Africa.

Finally, after tugging at the map and looking at it from every different angle, Aunt Jean buzzed the chauffeur and asked him how much longer he thought it would be to the elephant reserve.

"About one hour, Miss."

Aunt Jean looked pale. Liffey hesitated to ask but wanted to know the truth. "Aunt Jean, will we have enough money to pay the chauffeur when we get there? He might want cash."

"No, Liffey, I am afraid we will not. I forgot to exchange money at the airport."

"Not a problem, Aunt Jean. I have plenty. I hardly ever use my mother's trust account funds but I had some money transferred to my bank before we left and I *did* go to an ATM when you went to the luggage transfer office. Daddy always tells me to prepare for emergencies. So relax, Aunt Jean. Everything is under control."

A few minutes later, after they had turned on to a narrow, dusty road, a cape buffalo appeared directly in front of them followed by a calf trailing closely behind swinging its little tail back and forth like a metronome.

Aunt Jean squealed with delight. Liffey begged the chauffeur to stop so she could get her first safari video.

"I'll stop young lady, but you must take your pictures through the sun roof. You are not stepping out of this limo. Those are wild animals. We are not in a petting zoo."

Liffey opened the sunroof and stood up. With her head poking out, it was easy to aim her camcorder and zoom in on the buffalo family walking slowly down the road ahead of them.

Her eyes were suddenly drawn off the road, away from the buffalo.

A huge surge of adrenalin caused Liffey's legs to quiver and her arms to twitch as she tried to focus the camcorder on three female lions lying low in a crouching attack position behind two large rocks.

They were eyeing the little buffalo calf. It was clear to Liffey that they were looking for something to eat and planned to pounce on the baby buffalo and kill it.

Liffey heard a high pitched voice screaming, "Nooooo!" To her relief and astonishment, the lions jumped up and ran off into the underbrush.

The cape buffalo family hustled off the road to open ground where they were joined by the rest of their herd.

The buffalo calf was safe.

Liffey knew that she had completely disregarded what Aunt Jean had said was the most important rule of the bush: "*Never interfere with the wildlife.*"

She had totally interrupted Mother Nature when she had screamed at the lions but she could not just stand there watching while three big lions devoured a tiny buffalo calf.

"Thanks very much, Sir," Liffey said, sitting back down, ashamed that she had intervened but also exhilarated because she had saved the calf's life.

She hoped that the chauffeur had been wearing his earphones and had not heard her screaming at the lions.

Aunt Jean smiled gratefully.

"Thank you, Liffey."

"Lions need to know that they cannot just go around eating anything they please. They need to be put in their proper place."

"I have taken precautions to ensure that we will not become victims of their reckless eating habits."

Liffey had no idea what her aunt was talking about but said, "Thanks, Aunt Jean."

"It is really good to know that you are one step ahead of the lions."

chapter 12

ROBERT RIVERS READ the lake snake incident report his office had prepared for him while he sipped his morning coffee.

The security company which had installed the Rivers' alarm system discovered that there was a hole in the crawl space underneath the house which had probably been made by a groundhog.

It was their opinion that the snake was cold and had made its way into the house to warm itself. The hole was permanently sealed up.

A thorough background check had been done on Dr. Carl Carmichael. He checked out. Dr. Carmichael was an eccentric professor emeritus from the University of Chicago who had retired to Wisconsin.

Attorney Rivers instructed his staff to find out if Dr. Carmichael kept other exotic snakes along with Hannah and as far as anyone could tell, he did not.

As usual, the Rivers Law Office staff provided more information than expected or needed: 'The scientific name for King Cobra is *Ophiophagus hannah*. Ophiophagus means snake-eater in Latin.'

'Snake-Eater Hannah. Liffey would like that.' Robert Rivers smiled. 'Time to call her with an update on her mother's condition.'

✳ ✳ ✳

Liffey's phone was ringing but she was too stunned to answer it.

First, she would have to remember how to flip it open and then, how to open her mouth and speak.

At the moment she was speechless.

She was still trembling from witnessing the little buffalo's close brush with death by lion, and this 'camp' at the elephant reserve Aunt Jean had booked for the next six days was nothing more than a disguised luxury spa.

Liffey tried not to let on how disappointed she was because she could see that Aunt Jean was completely ecstatic.

"Liffey, darling, we can do the spa first thing in the morning. I can't wait to try the special camp Baobab Lotion. It's got something called Ferox Leaf in it and Neroli Aloe. Hmmm…I wonder if these would interact with my sunscreen?"

"Anyway, we are just in time for high tea, so let's freshen up a bit in our little step-down pool outside and then we can meet the other guests who will be riding with us in the bush. We get to choose our own elephant you know."

Liffey decided to read the Camp Ukuthula welcoming literature to find out what, if anything was going on here.

'They actually refer to this place as a *camp* in their brochure! That's where Aunt Jean picked up the 'camp' word,' thought Liffey, a little less angry now with her aunt who had apparently not meant to mislead her. Liffey realized that being in the middle of nowhere, even in a luxurious place like this, really was her aunt's idea of roughing it up in the wild.

Only Aunt Jean could have found such a bizarre place. There were nine luxury suites and a spa to 'wash away the stress.'

Each of the suites had an animal theme. They were staying in the Zebra Suite. It had three chairs made from real zebra skins and a bedspread with faux zebra skin. There were two pastel drawings of zebra grazing on savanna grasses, a poster of zebra with elephants and giraffes and an abstract oil painting of a mother zebra with a baby zebra.

Liffey googled 'zebra herd' and learned that a herd of zebra is called a 'dazzle.' She would have to tell this to Sinead.

❋ ❋ ❋

Aunt Jean left the suite to line up her stress relief treatment and to arrange their first elephant safari. As far as Liffey could tell after reading the Ukuthula brochure, you reserved an elephant here like you would reserve a horse at a riding stable.

❋ ❋ ❋

Shortly after arriving at Ukuthula, which according Aunt Jean was the Zulu word for 'peace,' Liffey checked their itinerary for next week's walking safari, hoping it was not going to be another 'stress relief' event.

Liffey was thrilled when she discovered that her aunt must have accidentally booked the wrong walking safari. Aunt Jean had signed them up for a no frills, four day *game* walk at a place called 'Camp Survival.'

This mistake most likely had happened because her aunt never paid attention to detail. There were quite a few walking safaris which advertised online. Aunt Jean must have become confused and impatiently selected one of them at random, thinking they were all basically the same.

Liffey smiled.

'Too bad Aunt Jean's attention span is about two seconds.'

'She thinks we are going to check into a five star tent lodge after this elephant spa and go on short walks each day. But we are really going to sleep in small tents with mosquito netting and sit around campfires and nap in hammocks. We will walk ten miles each day with an armed ranger and track the Big Five on foot.'

An excited shiver ran through Liffey as she pictured herself identifying lion tracks on the trail with the ranger.

Poor Aunt Jean.

chapter 13

SINEAD MCGOWAN RE-PACKED the open suitcase on her bed for the fourth time in her tiny Strandhill bedroom at the foot of Knocknarea.

She had never been to the States before and tried very hard not to show how excited she was so her older brothers would not tease her mercilessly about her unbridled enthusiasm.

As far as she could tell from the large map of Illinois and Wisconsin she had taped to her wall, Wisconsin looked like an interesting place. Liffey and she could go skiing at a man-made ski hill near the Rivers' house where machines made the snow for you if the winter weather was uncooperative.

Sinead was a bit worried about how Liffey was going to react to her mother's coming home again after all the years they had been apart.

'Thinking your mum is dead for most of your life and then finding out she's alive and you actually saw her once on an airplane and even hung out with her not knowing who she was, has got to be a hard thing to sort out.'

'It's weird how Liffey never mentions her mum when we talk and if I do, Liffey immediately changes the subject.'

Using a compass with Liffey's house in the center, she drew a circle around it with a radius of one hundred miles.

Madison, and Milwaukee in Wisconsin, and Chicago in Illinois, all fell within the circle. 'Definitely do Chicago,' Sinead thought.

'It was going to be an awesome trip.'

'If only this headache would go away…'

✳ ✳ ✳

The herper in Johannesburg carefully lifted the crate with Black Mamba from the back of a Mercedes truck parked in the almost empty car park under the Toyota Motors sign.

He could hear the snake thrashing around in the trap box. No wonder this snake was distressed. Was he dealing with a complete idiot? What kind of Cape Town herper would subject a snake to such primitive shipping conditions?

It must be dangerously overheated by now and very frightened. He would have to be extremely careful transferring this snake from the trap box into the twenty-foot cage he had prepared.

He respected the speed of this snake which the locals called, 'The Shadow of Death.'

The secrecy surrounding this snake pick-up was unusual and somewhat disturbing. He had received an anonymous letter in an envelope crammed full of diamonds with instructions to care for this snake until further notice and to make sure it was in excellent condition for an upcoming event.

Since Black Mamba could strike up to twelve times when provoked, the Johannesburg herper hoped that whoever was orchestrating this dangerous animal event knew what the consequences could be.

If it was going to be part of an illegal animal cage fight, the mamba would easily win.

✳ ✳ ✳

The Sisters had told Neil very little about how he had come to live with them in Johannesburg.

"You are a miracle sent from God," was their only explanation.

Now that he was older, Neil realized that what they actually meant was they had no idea where he had come from.

What he was most curious about was whether his parents had left him with the Sisters because he was crippled. Maybe they could not afford to care for him and thought the Sisters would be able to provide good medical care and find a doctor who could diagnose his condition.

Maybe the Sisters *would* fix him. Perhaps then his parents would come back and take him to live with them. Maybe he had brothers and sisters?

He was not certain, however, that he really wanted to leave.

Sister Helen and the others had been his family ever since he could remember.

He was happy.

✳ ✳ ✳

The Mercedes truck parked under the Toyota Motors sign was towed away from the car park at 1:00 p.m. to a recycling plant where it was immediately crushed and turned into scrap metal.

chapter 14

IT WAS HARD for Liffey to take the Ukuthula Elephant Reserve seriously because the elephants on the reserve were not wild. They had been raised by humans.

Just like she had done on the elephant rides at the zoo, Liffey climbed up rickety wooden stairs to a platform thirteen feet off the ground to reach the canvas-covered saddle on top of her elephant.

Each day like clockwork, the safari elephants walked on familiar trails, swaying back and forth, from side to side, like a group of zombies leaving a cemetery.

Liffey had been partnered with an elephant named 'Uthando.' One of the elephant handlers told her that 'Uthando' was the Zulu word for 'love.'

The only difference between the elephant-back safaris here at this reserve and the elephant rides at the zoo, was that at the zoo, the elephant was led around a large pen by a handler who had a rope attached to the animal.

Here at the elephant reserve, an armed ranger sat in front of Liffey like a body guard and gently guided Uthando along well worn trails.

As hard as she tried not to, Liffey usually fell asleep within ten minutes after Uthando set out each day, hypnotized by her elephant's pendulum-like gait.

Aunt Jean called these elephant treks 'communicating with the African bush.'

Liffey called them afternoon naps.

After four mid-afternoon siestas riding on her elephant, Liffey had only seen three zebra, two giraffes and one baboon. So far, the only Big Five animals she had spotted other than the tame elephants here on the reserve, were the cape buffalo on the entrance road to the camp and the crouching lions waiting to eat the baby buffalo.

Every night while Aunt Jean drank something called Sundowners and had a five course gourmet meal with china plates and sterling silver and crystal goblets, Liffey helped to feed and clean up after the elephants. It was the most interesting part of her day and she looked forward to her stable time while Aunt Jean was chattering away with people like herself who seemed to believe they really were having adventures and doing dangerous things together in the bush.

So far, the only dangerous thing Aunt Jean had done here at Camp Ukuthula was to apply her baobab body lotion over her sunscreen.

❋ ❋ ❋

Each elephant consumed almost six hundred pounds of grass each day and eliminated over three hundred pounds of dung, so the stable workers were happy to put Liffey to work.

She learned that elephants could live to be over fifty years old and grew six sets of teeth during their life spans. Liffey's elephant, Uthando, was smart. She could spray water from her trunk on command and make a pillow for herself out of hay before she went to sleep on the barn floor each night.

Even though Liffey remembered her father's advice to always "be careful what you wish for," she could not stop herself from wishing she and her aunt were already out of elephant land and on the walking safari. She desperately wanted some action.

The only thing to look forward to at Camp Ukuthula now was the final safari ride beginning at sunset tomorrow night when Liffey would ride Uthando for the last time after sunset.

✳ ✳ ✳

The darkly tanned man in an expensive white linen suit stood on his hotel balcony and chewed on a fat cigar trying to choose the right words before he made the call.

It was difficult not to be able to use his right hand to dial since he was right-handed. It would be weeks yet until the cast would be removed from his fractured right arm and he could stop wearing the uncomfortable neck brace.

He had never been sure that his command of the Afrikaans language was acceptable but his man here in Johannesburg did not speak English very well so he gave it a try:

"Die swart mamba is gereed. Ek sal jou binnekort kontak met die tyd en plek," he said in halting Afrikaans.

Next, in a smooth, cultured voice, he said in English:

"The black mamba is in place."

Then he ended the call.

Johannesburg was a done deal.

The snake was in place. Now it was just a matter of the small details.

It was regrettable that things had come to this but he knew Robert Rivers would eventually send his investigators to

Africa to put the Maeve McDermott-Mary Murphy puzzle pieces together and both mother and daughter were direct links to his diamond smuggling operation.

They could identify him.

When he was finished with the Rivers family, there would be no dots left connecting him with his diamonds.

chapter 15

AUNT JEAN WAS practicing how to walk using her trekking sticks while Liffey did her home school assignment of the day which was to stand out on their private viewing deck and look at the view.

Aunt Jean had further directed her to breathe deeply, close her eyes and meditate.

Liffey did not understand why her aunt did not see the contradiction here. How could she 'look at the view' if her eyes were closed while she meditated?

Aunt Jean also told Liffey to imagine she was face to face with a tiger while she was meditating so that if she actually did find herself face to face with a tiger tonight on the nighttime elephant safari, she would be prepared and not panic.

Liffey did not tell her aunt that there were no tigers in Africa. Instead, she imagined being face to face with a lion. She secretly hoped that this would not actually happen because she still thought about the Tsavo man-eater lions when the sun went down and she hoped none of the lions on this reserve were hungry tonight.

Aunt Jean had painted her fingernails white with black stripes to lure zebra and was wearing a giraffe patterned jacket to attract any giraffes that might be in the vicinity.

"Enough meditating, Liffey, darling! Did you look into the eye of the tiger, dear?"

Liffey said that she had.

"Good. Then we are ready! We shall take our tea now and eat plenty of cook's nourishing sandwiches. We will need all our strength tonight."

Liffey tried not to laugh. How much strength did someone need to ride around on the back of an elephant? And why was Aunt Jean acting like she was British or something?

"Take our tea?" Liffey wanted to ask her aunt where they should take it.

✳ ✳ ✳

After tea, Aunt Jean practiced with her snake hook back at the zebra suite and gave Liffey a lesson about what to do if they encountered a poisonous snake on their walking safari. 'Like she would know,' thought Liffey.

Liffey half listened to Aunt Jean talking about a dangerous snake her aunt called the black 'mambo.'

"Aunt Jean, a mambo is a Latin American dance step, not a snake." "Whatever," her aunt replied.

After the cobra incident in her living room, Liffey was dreading the prospect of meeting up with another slithering serpent.

Aunt Jean prattled on. "The black mambo is not really black, Liffey. It is 'gun metal grey' according to the videos I have watched."

"It is called the black mambo because the inside of its horrid mouth is black. When it swallows its meals, it collapses its jaws and can inhale any size animal. Even the fearless cape buffalo runs away from this terrifying snake."

"How could a 'mambo' eat a buffalo, Aunt Jean?"

"That is a very good question, Liffey," Aunt Jean said in her home school teacher's voice. "I am a conscientious educator so I will answer your question honestly."

"I do not know how the black mambo snake gets a huge cape buffalo into its mouth through its collapsed jaws. It is one of the mysteries of the bush."

Even though Liffey knew her Aunt Jean was crazy, and also knew that it was totally impossible for a snake to swallow a buffalo, the thought of a snake that could frighten something away that was a million times bigger than itself was very disconcerting.

Aunt Jean continued. "We will be walking one mile a day on the nature safari we are embarking upon tomorrow, Liffey. One half mile out into the bush where we will observe the flowers and birds and other wild life and then one half mile back to camp where we will relax and get ready for the next grueling day."

"Safaris are not easy, Liffey. They are every bit as demanding as feiseanna."

"Speaking of which, we must remember to point our toes as we are walking along the trails tomorrow. We must not lose our competitive edge before the Johannesburg Feis. We will practice our leapovers when we encounter dangerous snakes. I shall use my hook to discourage those snakes we do not wish to leap over and drive them back into the bush."

Aunt Jean unfastened her bulky bathrobe and pretended that its long, blue tie was a snake. Then she hooked the tie and demonstrated how she would handle a poisonous snake.

Liffey exhaled. Soon Aunt Jean would realize they were not going to be pampered anymore.

She hoped her aunt would cope and not start fainting and having little nervous breakdowns tomorrow at Camp Survival.

✳ ✳ ✳

Sinead smiled. It was hard not to let on to Liffey's father that Liffey and her Aunt Jean were in Africa on safari but she had promised she would not tell.

"It's not a lie, Sinead, if you just don't bring the subject up. Daddy worries about me too much."

Liffey's texts from Africa were very exciting. Especially the one about riding her elephant at night:

"omg! I saw sooo many animals...lions, zebra, 2 leopards, 3 snakes, bats, monster rhino, hyenas. AJ says smell of elephants keeps rhinos away. hippo eyes in river looking at me. 5 giraffes sleeping on ground. Camp Survival tomorrow. AJ will completely freak out. no spa. no toilets. no nothing."

✳ ✳ ✳

Sinead popped two Panadol capsules into her mouth and reached for her bottled water. 'Four hours of waiting for the next dose is too long for a headache this bad.'

She reached over the hospital bed rail and patted Maeve Rivers' limp hands which were folded together like she was praying. Suddenly, Mrs. Rivers' hands became rigid and her eyes popped open like she was possessed. She looked directly at Sinead with a terrified expression and cried out:

"Die swart mamba is gereed!"

Sinead tried not to look as alarmed as she felt and said, "Don't be afraid. Your husband will be right back, Mrs. Rivers. You can tell him all about it and I am sure he will be able to make you feel better."

She picked up the small notebook Attorney Rivers kept on the bed stand to jot down anything Maeve said that he thought might be important. Sinead had no idea what Mrs. Rivers had said. It sounded like gibberish but might have been another language.

"Dee swahrt mam bah is gah reed."

"Is that what you said, Mrs. Rivers?"

'I wonder what language this is?' Sinead knew a little German because she often helped her friend Mairead prepare for German quizzes. The words Mrs. Rivers had just shouted out sounded like German or maybe Dutch. One of Mairead's quizzes had been about colors and she was fairly certain that 'schwarz' was the word for black in German. But Mrs. Rivers did not say 'schwarz.' There was no 'Z' sound, just a hard 'T.'

The word 'mamba' might mean a mamba snake.

'Was Mrs. Rivers talking about a black mamba snake in this mysterious language and if so, why?'

All this word deciphering was making today's headache worse and trying to write legibly in the notebook was making her right hand spasm.

The Extra Strength Panadol she had taken one hour ago had not helped much.

She looked at her watch. Three more hours and she could take two more pills.

One of these days she would have to tell her parents about this constant headache. But not until she got back from the States.

They might not let her go if they thought something might be seriously wrong with her.

chapter 16

It was 7:30 a.m. Liffey could not decide whether or not she should warn Aunt Jean that they were not on their way to another luxury spa. She was leaning towards not bringing the subject up and waiting to see what would happen.

The jeep they were riding in should have clued her aunt in. It needed new shocks. Every bump they went over felt like their bottoms were smacking against hard cement. Aunt Jean wore a fixed smile to show it was not bothering her but Liffey could tell she was in pain.

"Aunt Jean, why don't we sit on some of these old newspapers and magazines that are piled up on the floor? They would cushion the bumps a little." Aunt Jean agreed. They stacked up inches of cushioning papers under them and Aunt Jean's frozen smile turned into a real one shortly thereafter.

"I just don't understand this vehicle, Liffey, darling. I knew the camp was sending a driver and assumed it would probably not be an air conditioned limo but I never expected to ride in a rusted out, roofless jeep with bald tires."

"What if we have a flat? There are beasts everywhere lurking in the bush just waiting for such an event. We could be eaten."

Liffey assured her aunt that the driver carried a gun. She could see it strapped to a holster around his waist. There was also a high powered rifle on the front passenger seat next to him.

"If a beast tries to eat us, I am sure the driver will save us, Aunt Jean."

"I suppose you're right Liffey, dear. All I need is a good massage and a nice cool bath as soon as we arrive at Camp Serenity."

Liffey slunk down guiltily in her seat.

Camp Serenity?

'That must be where Aunt Jean thinks we are going. She must have clicked on 'Camp Survival' instead of 'Camp Serenity' when she booked our tour. Bad mistake. Aunt Jean really needs to learn how to concentrate. I don't know how I am going to tell her.'

The jeep came to a complete stop for a huge mother elephant crossing the road with her baby, padding along underneath her.

Mr. Powers, the jeep's driver, who had hardly spoken a word so far, perked up a bit and said, "Most animal species here give birth to their young during the rainy season. Keep still, ladies. Don't talk until Lady Elephant is out of sight."

The mother elephant stopped in the middle of the road while her calf strolled out from under her over to a thicket of acaia trees and began to strip the leaves off the lowest branches.

"Acaia trees are elephants' favorite food, ladies. We may be sitting here for some time while they snack."

Liffey noted the look of horror on her aunt's face.

"Can't you drive around the mother elephant, Mr. Powers?" Liffey asked. Aunt Jean had begun to sweat profusely in the early morning heat.

Mr. Powers replied, "Baby elephants stay no more than fifteen feet away from their mothers for eight years. If I try to get around mama, she might get worried and charge at us."

Before Liffey could continue, there was a rumbling beneath the jeep, like a faraway freight train coming closer and closer.

"It sounds like there's a herd of elephants coming this way, ladies."

Aunt Jean dug her striped zebra finger nails into Liffey's arm.

"How many elephants are in a herd, Liffey?"

"I'm not sure, Aunt Jean. I think usually around thirty."

The driver was reading a book about fly fishing in Colorado, waiting for the mother elephant to decide to go to the other side of the road before the herd arrived.

Aunt Jean was clinging to Liffey like they were going to be eaten in the wild at any second. Even Liffey was becoming somewhat nervous because the ground underneath them was beginning to feel like an earthquake.

Suddenly the mother elephant reared up making loud trumpeting sounds and faced the jeep head on.

The driver tensed and drew his gun from its holster, reminding Liffey that he was a trained ranger.

"Not to worry ladies. I have been through this before. She wants to intimidate us a bit. Probably having a bad day. Thinks we might harm her baby. Sit perfectly still. Do not move. Most likely, she will kick up her heels a bit and move towards us. If she charges, I will take immediate evasive action and shoot if I have to."

Aunt Jean went limp and slumped down on Liffey's shoulder.

'So much for practicing how to be terrified in the bush,' Liffey thought. Liffey had seen her aunt have fainting spells before and thought that they had often looked suspicious, like Aunt Jean was either faking or exaggerating. Now, however, Liffey could see that her aunt had actually passed out.

She slipped her arm around Aunt Jean's waist and lifted her head up to support it. Maybe it was just as well that Aunt Jean had completely tuned out. Liffey was beginning to become very apprehensive feeling the ground vibrations escalate. When the jeep itself began to shake, it sounded like hundreds of elephants would soon be upon them.

Aunt Jean was completely helpless. 'How many elephants could a ranger handle at the same time?' Shooting at the poor elephants would be horrifying. It was not the elephants' fault that this safari jeep was driving on their turf.'

'TURF!!'

"How could I be so dense?" Liffey shouted to Mr. Powers.

She repositioned Aunt Jean on the seat and reached into a zipped up compartment in her backpack for a package wrapped in aluminum foil which contained several lumps of dried elephant dung mixed with ground up chili peppers.

Liffey had asked the cooks at the elephant reserve for some chili peppers after she had watched a travelogue about elephant trunks being extremely sensitive to capsaicin, the chemical that makes red chili peppers hot.

Farmers in South Africa burned these peppers mixed with elephant dung to keep elephants out of their crop fields at night. While Aunt Jean dined and played card games every night, Liffey made three dung bombs to bring along on the game tracking safari just in case they met up with a rogue male elephant. She had not expected an angry mother elephant.

"Excuse me, Mr. Powers. I think I can help here. Do you have a match or lighter?"

Mr. Powers did not respond. He looked like a cowboy waiting for a shoot out in a Wild West saloon.

"I have three chili peppers dung logs to burn," Liffey said. "We could put two of them right outside the jeep facing in the direction the wind is blowing which I think is the direction the elephants are coming at us from."

"The other one we could put on the hood of the jeep to ward off the mother. When she reacts, we will have our chance to drive around her."

"The herd should pick up the pepper scent quickly and not risk charging us until the scent is gone. Elephants hate red pepper smoke. They can smell way better than we do so the herd will try to get as far away from the pepper smoke as possible."

Mr. Powers looked distraught and still said nothing so Liffey crawled over the back seat up to the front where she found a lighter on the dash board.

Mr. Powers remained mute and looked skulled so Liffey leaned over and carefully placed one log on the hood of the jeep between them and the mother elephant. Then she flicked on the lighter and ignited it.

"I will place the other two logs outside the jeep when the mother's ears start flapping and she starts to leave," she informed Mr. Powers.

The ranger continued to stare at the mother elephant, transfixed. Liffey strongly suspected this might be his first encounter with an elephant that was ready to charge a jeep.

She grabbed a newspaper to fan the clouds of smoke rising from the hood of the jeep towards the mother elephant.

Finally, the mother's ears flared out and she began to shake her head back and forth, making high pitched trumpeting sounds as she turned away from the jeep and pounded across the road towards her baby.

The two of them stampeded off into the dense brush.

Liffey sighed. "Well at least we have more logs if we meet up with any more mad elephants."

The relieved ranger floored the accelerator and tore off in a cloud of dust and red pepper dung smoke.

Liffey climbed into the back seat again with Aunt Jean and rearranged their safari hats to block the intense rays from the South African sun.

Soon they would be at Camp Survival.

chapter 17

NEIL PULLED HIMSELF up using the bedrails on each side of him. He had been having difficulty sleeping for the past week.

He did not tell Sister Helen because she would make him drink warm milk before he went to bed and warm milk always made him gag.

There had been nightmares. Dark shadows of snakes on the face of a bright full moon. Long snakes biting his legs…

If he told Sister Helen about these dreams, she would worry about him.

He switched on the overhead light using the long string attached to the light's pull cord and then immediately shut his eyes because the string and cord cast a long shadow on the wall next to him like a moving snake.

Maybe if he kept the lights on and did not fall asleep in the dark, the dreams would not come again tonight.

✳ ✳ ✳

It was hard for Robert Rivers not to accidentally slip up and tell Liffey that Sinead was coming back with Maeve and him to Wisconsin. Sinead had given her word not to tell Liffey and ruin the surprise.

For the past three months, Sinead had come to the hospital almost every day after school to sit with Maeve while he ran errands and networked with his Chicago law office. She refused to take any money for what was technically a babysitting job.

Liffey was right when she referred to Sinead as her mother's personal guardian angel.

Recently, Attorney Rivers had become concerned about Sinead. She looked pale and it was obvious that she had lost a good bit of weight. And, although she never complained, he could tell she was often in pain.

When he asked Sinead if she were ill and if he could help, all she said was, "Don't worry Mr. Rivers, it's just a plugged up sinus condition."

A Rivers Law Office investigator had sent Sinead's notes to a language expert who thought that the sounds Sinead had written down when she was alone with Maeve were Afrikaans words and the translated sentence was: "The black mamba is in place."

Attorney Rivers wondered if Sinead's sinus condition was affecting her hearing. The 'black mamba' phrase made no sense. The only black mamba he could think of was a snake. Maybe Maeve had seen one in Africa.

❊ ❊ ❊

Aunt Jean woke up shortly after the elephant crisis had passed and thanked Mr. Powers for saving their lives. He turned around, smiled humbly and said, "It's my job. It was a privilege, Ms. Rivers."

Aunt Jean gushed, "Well I think you are a hero, Mr. Powers and I will always be eternally grateful to you for risking your own life to save ours."

Aunt Jean poked Liffey hard in the ribs to remind her to chime in with her own thank you.

"I too will be eternally grateful, Mr. Powers. I don't know what we would have done without you."

✳ ✳ ✳

A small buffalo thorn tree stood next to a pile of rocks on top of a vacant termite hill where the black mamba was sunbathing. Light yellow blossoms on the tree branches were beginning to be replaced by small brown berries.

For three days the black mamba had been gorging on the birds eating the insects on the tree's ripening fruit.

Rarely had the black mamba found so much food with so little effort.

Life was easy.

✳ ✳ ✳

Black Mamba was sleeping on a large tree branch inside a twenty foot cage.

Every twelve hours a large mouse was released from a small holding cell into the cage.

Black Mamba quickly injected its venom into these mice and immobilized them instantly. They felt no pain because the neurotoxins in Black Mamba's venom immediately shut down their tiny nervous systems and the cardiotoxins stopped their hearts in five seconds.

Hunting for prey was like driving through a fast food restaurant.

Life was easy.

chapter 18

"IT IS NOW time for you to memorize the names of the creatures which belong to the 'Little Five,' Liffey," Aunt Jean said as she reached into her bag for her notes.

"The Little Five?"

This was the first time Liffey had heard about there being a 'Little Five.' Aunt Jean was using her School of Life Home School teacher's voice and Liffey worried again that her aunt might have a major meltdown when she discovered where they were really going.

"Yes, Liffey, the Little Five are: the Dung Beetle, the Ant Lion, the Leopard Tortoise, the Elephant Shrew and the Buffalo Weaver."

"Monsieur Poinsette told me that if we were going on a nature trail safari, we needed to learn the names of the Little Five."

Liffey was becoming concerned.

"Who is Monsieur Poinsette, Aunt Jean?"

"He is a concierge at Camp Ukuthula and an experienced trekker. He said at Camp Serenity we will study dung beetles and ant lions and if we are really fortunate, perhaps we will see a leopard tortoise and an elephant shrew as well."

"Apparently we can only hope to see a buffalo weaver as we trek along the trails, Liffey. They are rare. From now on, we will be exploring the wilderness on foot."

"No more elephants transporting us on dangerous Big Five game drives each day. We will soon be observing spiders and ants and termites and many more of the little creatures which we so often walk right by without so much as a nod or kind word."

"What are you talking about, Aunt Jean? Why would we want to talk to bugs?"

"Liffey, darling, at Camp Serenity we will search for peace of mind. This is, after all, a Christmas safari. We will observe how heaven and nature sing together in unison at this joyful time of year. Mother Earth is full of bugs, Liffey. It is high time we made an effort to get to know them."

'Maybe I had better give Daddy a call and let him know where we are,' Liffey worried. 'Aunt Jean is beginning to freak me out. She is making no sense whatsoever. When she figures out we will be tracking lions and not trekking along looking for bugs, she might completely check out.'

'I should have asked the feis doctor in New York if going on a safari would be too much for her. Tracking the Big Five is a bit more stressful than observing dung beetles and she did not exactly handle the elephant crisis on the road very well. She was passed out for fifteen minutes.'

"Mr. Powers, can you please tell me how much longer to camp?" Liffey asked.

"About twenty minutes, Miss Rivers," he replied.

Liffey fervently hoped that Camp Survival did not have a sign at the entrance announcing its intentions. It was only a matter of a very short time now before Aunt Jean would discover what she was in for.

'I hope she does not decide to pack up and make us leave,' Liffey thought anxiously. After six days of riding elephants on automatic pilot, Liffey was more than ready to learn how to survive in the wild.

The jeep began to navigate narrow, twisty roads which reminded Liffey of dirt bike trails.

The land had become a grassy plain and the horizon was completely flat with a few scattered trees. Finally, Mr. Powers stopped the jeep at a dead end which had a small cul-de-sac and began to unload their large backpacks.

After Liffey insisted that bringing their luggage along on the walking safari would be crazy, Aunt Jean sent it on to Johannesburg to the hotel where they would be staying during the feis.

Camp Survival had no sign posted and was not gated. There was no one in sight to welcome them.

Mr. Powers cheerfully removed their stuffed backpacks from the jeep and handed them to Liffey and Aunt Jean. Liffey also carried Aunt Jean's oversized bag full of lotions and makeup. She had been unable to convince her aunt that wearing makeup while walking in the hot sun was not a good idea.

"The eyes are the mirror of the soul, Liffey. If I do not enlarge my eyes with liner and apply mascara to extend my lashes, my soul might remain hidden from the creatures in the bush."

Liffey did not have a comeback remark so she had dropped the subject. It was never really possible to convince her aunt of anything if she had already made her mind up about something.

A sudden clap of thunder and rolling black clouds reminded Liffey that it rained here in the summer. Sometimes, the month of December had as much as five inches. It had been dry all week at camp Ukuthula and this sudden warning of an imminent downpour was startling.

Before Liffey could ask Mr. Powers if they should put on their rain gear, he stopped and said: "Let's suit up in our water repellant clothing ladies before we get soaked. We have three miles to walk yet."

"I beg your pardon, Mr. Powers," Aunt Jean said impatiently, searching for her rain gear, "three miles to walk where?"

"To the camp, Ms. Rivers," Mr. Powers replied.

"Why are we not *driving* in your little jeep to our camp?"

"Because there is no road left to drive on, Miss Rivers."

"Why ever not, Mr. Powers?"

"Well I suppose the resident wildlife just never got around to building one."

"You expect us to walk three miles through the bush? We might be eaten Mr. Powers!"

'Oh no,' thought Liffey. 'It has begun. I should have told Aunt Jean she booked the wrong camp. It is going to be a very long four days.'

❊ ❊ ❊

Approximately fifty yards into the high savanna grasses, a hard, pelting rain began. Aunt Jean screamed, "Liffey, I thought Africa was a dry place! What is going on?"

"In the summer it rains here a lot Aunt Jean."

"What do you mean summer? It's Christmas!"

"It's summer here now, Aunt Jean. Not winter like back in Wisconsin."

Liffey could see that Aunt Jean was very upset and confused upon receiving this bad news. 'Why then did she order all the waterproof gear if she did not think it was going to rain here on safari?'

"Aunt Jean, this heavy rain is good because it will keep all the wild animals away from us because they will be taking shelter."

The downpour was over almost as quickly as it had begun and the sun blasted the earth again, drying the open grassland.

"Keep an eye out for snakes, ladies," Mr. Powers advised.

"What does he mean keep an eye out for snakes, Liffey?"

"I think he means keep an eye out for snakes, Aunt Jean. There are lots of snakes here in Africa."

"Does he mean right here where we are walking, Liffey?"

"I don't know, Aunt Jean. If Mr. Powers said to watch out for snakes, he probably means just keep your eyes open and watch out for them."

"What do we do if we actually see a snake, Liffey?"

"I guess we just try to avoid it, Aunt Jean."

"How?"

Liffey sighed. This was going to be a very long four day walking safari.

❋ ❋ ❋

"All right, ladies. We need to discuss a few things before we go any further," Mr. Powers said as he secured his Winchester rifle belt on his shoulder.

"This is where the real safari begins. We are about to begin walking through large areas of unspoiled wilderness on foot. We will most likely see many free-roaming animals on their own ground. Remember, this is their home, not ours. This is not a theme park and the animals here are not tame."

"From this point on we will no longer speak to one another. We will walk single file, arm's length apart, in silence. If you need to stop, click your tongue or snap your fingers. Do whatever works for you."

"Do not talk."

"If I raise my arm with a closed fist, you must stop immediately and freeze in place. Whatever you do, do not make a sound or move when you see my fist in the air. All of the Big Five inhabit this territory as do many other dangerous animals."

"It is extremely unlikely that any of these animals will cross our path because they will smell us from far away and seek to avoid us. But should the exception to this rule occur, remember this is not a zoo. These are wild, deadly animals and must be treated with great caution."

"As a last resort, I have been trained to use this rifle and will do so if I determine it to be necessary."

Liffey could feel Aunt Jean's fingernails making permanent dents in her right arm.

"What if I have to sneeze or cough, Liffey?"

"Then I guess you just sneeze or cough, Aunt Jean. People go on walking safaris all the time and I am sure many of them sneeze and cough without immediately being eaten alive afterwards."

❈ ❈ ❈

Aunt Jean did not complain or whine or react to anything at all for the next two miles. Even when Mr. Powers silently pointed out two giraffes standing directly ahead of them eating leaves from a buffalo thorn tree where the grass ended and a clump of thick vegetation began.

She walked directly behind Liffey as instructed and touched Liffey's shoulder blades approximately every one hundred feet or so to make sure she was always exactly one arm's length behind.

Mr. Powers kept a steady pace and both Liffey and her aunt fell into a comfortable stride with him.

'Aunt Jean is not freaking out,' Liffey thought happily. 'Maybe I have been too hard on her and she isn't going to completely wimp out on this safari after all. She seems to be following Mr. Powers' directions.'

Liffey turned her head around to give Aunt Jean an encouraging smile.

Aunt Jean did not look up. She was busy texting and listening to music. It apparently had not occurred to her that it might be a good idea to keep a sharp lookout on a game trail in South Africa.

'Why should Aunt Jean take in the sights here in Africa when she could be listening to 'The Lion Sleeps Tonight' and texting her lame clown alley friends instead?'

chapter 19

NEIL LIKED MONDAYS. On Monday mornings from 8:00 a.m. until 10:30 a.m. he had the inside therapy pool all to himself without interruption. Robert, his hydro therapist, worked with him in the water for the first forty-five minutes after which he was free to swim on his own.

Neil's breaststroke had become very strong and Sister Helen talked about the possibility of his swimming competitively in school someday. Sister Helen thought he could do anything. She had not considered the small detail of his not being able to dive into his pool lane for a good start and then having to push off with his arms instead of his legs for the turnaround on the other side of the pool.

In the pool, Neil sometimes imagined that his legs were moving and not just floating on the ripples he created with his upper body. Sister Helen believed in visualization. "See your legs moving in the water, Neil. Be open to the possibility that one day your legs will work properly."

Later today he would have to practice violin again for the Johannesburg Feis this Saturday. It wasn't that he did not know his music. He wanted to build up stamina.

He did not want to hinder a dancer because he might become tired and begin to get sloppy. He had to be precise and play with authority so the dancers could do their best. He would be playing for the beginner stages where there were often dancers competing for their first time at a feis. He was determined to make the experience as easy and pleasant as possible.

✳ ✳ ✳

The Johannesburg herper received a call to return Black Mamba to the same parking lot where he had picked the snake up. He was to leave the picnic basket in back of a white Lexis which would be parked under the Toyota Motors sign. This secrecy bothered him a great deal but he was already in too deep to ask any questions now since he had already cashed in the diamonds and deposited a large sum of money in an off shore bank account.

He suspected that whoever was orchestrating this stupid snake joke might be a very dangerous person. He decided he did not want to find out just how dangerous and began to follow the instructions to prepare a large picnic basket for the fourteen foot snake for a 6:45 a.m. delivery on Saturday morning.

Leaving a poisonous snake in an unlocked white Lexis for a stranger to pick up was probably a crime in itself but there was no way he was going to stick around and meet the person or persons who wanted this snake. He would do exactly what he was told to do and get out of there as fast as he could.

✳ ✳ ✳

The hotel room phone was ringing. The handsome young man buffing his brown leather shoes answered it. Black Mamba was to be picked up at 7:00 a.m. Saturday morning at the same place he had originally deposited the snake, in the car park under the Toyota Motors sign.

Black Mamba would be in the back of a white Lexis inside a large picnic hamper fastened tightly with a six inch leather strap. He was to proceed with great caution as the snake would not have been fed for thirty hours prior to the pickup and would be ravenous.

Further instructions would be in an envelope tucked under the leather strap along with the keys to the Lexis.

He was to leave the blue Ford rental car under the Toyota Motors sign.

✸ ✸ ✸

Sinead closed her suitcase, satisfied at last that she had packed enough clothing for three weeks in the States. Even though she and Liffey both wore size 'small,' she was at least four inches taller than Liffey so she could not count on wearing Liffey's clothes as a backup. They would not fit properly.

Since she wore a uniform to school each day, she did not have many outfits when she began to pack. Thanks to her friends at the Ursuline College who had loaned her some of their sweaters and accessories, and clearance sales in Sligo Town, she would look presentable. Better than presentable. She would look good. Besides, Liffey would not care in the least how she dressed.

Liffey was far more interested in stirring things up around her than worrying about what someone was wearing.

Sinead knew she had to tell someone soon about her constant headache. It was not normal and she was becoming exhausted from trying to hide the tremor in her right hand. If she told her parents, they would never permit her to go to the States until they were sure she was all right and Doctor Dorman would immediately admit her for tests at Sligo General or maybe even send her off to Galway or Dublin.

Sinead knew deep down that she was not well. Something bad was going on inside her head. Whatever it was, it would have to keep until she came back from her trip.

✳ ✳ ✳

The medical transport flight plan from Mayo's Knock International Airport to Chicago was finalized. From Chicago, Maeve would be transported by ambulance back to Wisconsin and the lake home she had designed before Liffey was born. Robert Rivers was ecstatic. He had long ago stopped dreaming that this day would ever come. He texted Liffey with the good news, making sure not to let on that Sinead McGowan would be waiting for her in Wisconsin too.

✳ ✳ ✳

Sam Snyder dreaded the return of his employer. He had not been completely honest with him. He *had* told Attorney Rivers that his sister and daughter had gone to a feis in New York. He had *not* told him that they had boarded a flight to South Africa and had not returned to Wisconsin.

After he had accessed Jean Rivers' credit card files on her computer, he learned they were headed to Johannesburg, South Africa. He located them at the Camp Ukuthula elephant reserve.

Attorney Rivers had authorized him to spend any amount of money necessary to protect his family while he was gone so he immediately contacted a detective agency in Johannesburg and they dispatched an Agent Powers to watch them from a distance at Ukuthula after which he was to supervise them at their next destination, Camp Survival.

Detective Powers was a retired Kruger National Park Ranger. He was told not to let the ladies out of his sight.

chapter 20

AUNT JEAN WAS thinking about the surprise solo dress she had designed for Liffey for the Johannesburg Feis.

The buffalo thorn tree design on the orange cape had been a brilliant last minute inspiration. Liffey would like the idea that buffalo thorn trees often mark the graves of Zulu chiefs.

She hoped Liffey would like the leopard fringe trim and the lion mane solo dress crown with tiny plastic cape buffalo horns.

She knew it was risky not getting Liffey's input about such a bold design concept but Liffey was young and inexperienced in the fashion world.

To make sure Liffey would have the courage to wear this safari look solo dress, Aunt Jean had switched solo dresses in Liffey's dress carrier.

The blue solo dress made in Ireland that Liffey had designed was now hanging in a closet in Wisconsin.

✳ ✳ ✳

"Camp Survival, ladies," Mr. Powers announced.

Liffey looked right. Then she looked left. Then she looked behind her. There was nothing to look at other than the same tall grass and scrub brush they had been walking through for the past hour and a half.

"How can you tell that this is Camp Survival, Mr. Powers?" Liffey asked with genuine interest.

Aunt Jean continued to text and listen to music. Liffey wondered if her aunt had even heard Mr. Powers announce that they had reached their destination.

"Do you see the three buffalo thorn trees standing in a row straight ahead?"

"Yes, I do, Mr. Powers," Liffey answered.

"That's how I can tell."

Liffey was beginning to feel a bit anxious.

Was Camp Survival going to be like one of those television shows where people got dumped on an island and had to forage for food and make their own huts?

Liffey was not sure she wanted to spend time doing that kind of thing. She wanted to learn how to track the Big Five and then sleep in a tent on a cot after sitting around a campfire each night.

Aunt Jean finally looked up from texting and said, "Are we lost, Mr. Powers? Would you like to use my GPS to help you find the camp?"

Before he could reply that he would much rather use three buffalo thorn trees than a mobile phone's global positioning system, far off in the distance, he saw three horses moving towards them.

He pointed out the approaching horses. "The riders will dismount here and continue on foot to the jeep we left behind in the cul-de-sac. We will mount their horses and ride to the hub of Camp Survival."

"On the fourth day, we will ride the same horses back here to these buffalo thorn trees, switch with new campers and then walk back to the jeep and drive to a landing strip where a small plane will pick us up and take us to Johannesburg."

"By then, you ladies will most probably be ready to re-enter civilization and get a big steak at the Carnivore Restaurant."

❊ ❊ ❊

"Why does he keep calling Camp Serenity, Camp Survival, Liffey?"

Liffey shrugged her shoulders so she did not have to lie out loud.

❊ ❊ ❊

"These are South African Boerperd horses, ladies," Mr. Powers said after the three riders had dismounted and set out on foot for the jeep.

"This breed was developed here in South Africa. These horses are sturdy, intelligent and good natured. We will ride them to our base camp."

"Give them plenty of rein and make sure your helmets fit snugly," Mr. Powers advised, adjusting their stirrups. Then he slung their backpacks over the long shoulders of each of the beautiful horses and mounted his chocolate brown mare.

Liffey was thrilled.

So far, Camp Survival had been one surprise after another.

Aunt Jean appeared to be very happy and patted her chestnut horse's head affectionately.

Except for the rifle which was still belted to Mr. Powers' shoulder, there was no hint of impending danger as the three riders struck out across the tall grass.

chapter 21

THE BLACK MAMBA slithered out of its underground lair in the old termite mound to the top of the small hill where hundreds of noisy birds were feasting on the ripening berries of a tiny buffalo thorn tree growing in the center of the knoll. The morning sun warmed the mamba's body quickly. Soon it would have the strength to take its first prey.

❊ ❊ ❊

Liffey was beginning to feel like she was a part of Africa as she rode along on the savanna plains.

Her horse's name was Leo. "Short for Leonardo," Mr. Powers told her. Leo was very grey and very calm.

Every so often he would stop and munch some grass but then move forward again without any prodding.

Not far ahead there was a small tree sitting on top of a large beehive shaped mound.

Liffey watched as hundreds of birds circled the tree like a squadron of airplanes nose diving into its fragrant branches. Next to the tree was a pile of rocks which reminded Liffey of a mini Queen Maeve's cairn.

When Mr. Powers' horse reached the small hill, it unexpectedly reared up spooked and then bolted away completely out of control.

Aunt Jean's horse also panicked and followed Mr. Powers' horse.

Following suit, Leonardo began bucking wildly and threw Liffey to the ground. Then he was off in pursuit of the other two horses before Liffey knew what had happened.

Shaken and dazed, Liffey sat up slowly. She had only had a split second to decide whether or not she should hold on to the reins and try to get control back of Leonardo or to let go of them instead and not risk becoming entangled in them. She had managed to get her feet out of the stirrups before she fell and had gone down properly, curling up like a hedgehog as she had been taught to do in a riding class two years ago.

She shielded her face from the glaring sun. She could see that Leonardo was gone. Her throbbing head felt as if it weighed a hundred pounds and sweat was pouring down her face and neck from under her protective helmet.

'What had come over all three of those wonderful, intelligent and good natured whatever they were called horses?' Liffey thought, holding back the tears of frustration she felt welling up inside her eyes.

She looked around on the ground underneath her and saw that she was sitting next to a small hole leading into the base of a small beehive shaped hill. She wondered if something lived in there.

'I must have a concussion,' Liffey thought, taking off her helmet and massaging her forehead with both hands, 'because I am hearing that same hissing noise like the sound the cobra made in my living room.' It seemed to be coming from the top of the mound. The birds had left the tree and except for the hissing, it was quiet.

Liffey tried not to panic. She had a concussion. The hissing had to be coming from inside of her ears even though it sounded like it was coming from the top of the little hill.

The sun was blinding her and it was impossible to clearly see what was up there.

When she shielded her eyes with her riding helmet, she was able to make out a long, slim form raised up at least four feet from the ground. It was watching her.

Her eyes slowly went into focus and she could see a large black mouth and flattened, coffin shaped head. It was a black mamba.

The most lethal snake in Africa was going to strike at her like a bolt of lightning before she could even get up off the ground and then she would be dead.

Liffey's life began to flash by her like a spilled jigsaw puzzle.

She saw her father's kind eyes and Aunt Jean's stuffed clothes closet and poor little Max.

Who was going to take care of Max the Magnificent? He slobbered too much and he always needed to go outside.

There was a diamond 'M' necklace around the neck of a woman with a beautiful smile and Sinead laughing and Principal Godzilla's squeaky athletic shoes walking down a school hallway.

Liffey knew the drill.

Don't move.

Don't breathe.

Stay perfectly still.

A snake will go away if it thinks it is not being threatened.

There were no faraway sounds of approaching horse hooves. She was completely alone here with a huge black mamba snake hissing at her from not quite ten feet away.

'*Deja vu*,' Liffey thought, remembering the terrifying thud on her living room door just as she slammed it shut. There was no door to slam shut here. No 911 number to call to get help.

This snake was not backing down and moving away from her in the opposite direction like it was supposed to do if you remained perfectly still. It was clearly very alarmed and getting ready for a preemptive strike.

Her canteen with the ground up book particles from Ireland was tied to her pack on Leonardo's back.

She would have no Saint Patrick's blessing if the snake bit her.

"So much for being prepared," Liffey cried out hopelessly.

The snake hissed again and did a menacing test lunge.

"Like I really want to fight with you," Liffey muttered under her breath almost laughing, trying not to give in to the rapidly mounting, complete panic surging though her.

Liffey was still shocked and dazed from her hard fall from the horse. It was difficult for her to sort out her thoughts and take action.

She couldn't even manage to do the hat trick her father had taught her a long time ago to regain control of things when everything seemed hopeless and impossible: "Bend over to pick up your thinking cap and then put it back on your head so you can think clearly again." Liffey knew she dared not move even an inch so she imagined putting the thinking cap back on her head.

The mamba lunged a second time.

The thinking cap trick was starting to work. She remembered reading that the black mamba was not aggressive unless something was blocking its way back to where it lived. Mambas inhabited the same place for many years unless something or someone disturbed their habitat.

The small hole in the hill Liffey was sitting right next to now could very well be the entrance to this mamba's home.

She needed to get *away* from this hole. When the snake lunged a third time, it was clear it was going to strike soon. She dared not stand up and began to slowly back away from the hill on her bottom.

It seemed to work. The snake did not lunge again. Instead it lowered itself and then vanished from the top of the hill. It was obviously retreating!

Liffey stood up and allowed herself to breathe easily again as she moved quickly in the opposite direction. She was relieved her legs seemed to be working properly after the fall.

Something made her turn around for one last look at the hill.

Hundreds of noisy birds were congregating on the low tree branches again completely unaware that one of them could easily be the next meal for the black mamba that lived under the termite hill.

Liffey was staring at the birds thinking that perhaps she should put more distance between herself and the snake when the black mamba came into view again from around the back of the hill.

It was moving fast.

Liffey did not have time to react. This snake would strike at her in seconds if she did not flee for her very life right now.

Liffey's feet began to move under her. It no longer mattered where the horses were or in what direction she should run. She needed to get as far away from the mamba as she possibly could.

After barely a minute of running, Liffey realized she would have to conserve her energy under the torrid mid-day African sun or she might get heat stroke. It had to be in the 90's.

She stopped, gasping for air and looked behind her again. 'No snake could keep up with me moving at this speed.'

The tall grass was moving about fifty feet away when the snake's head suddenly popped up like a submarine's periscope surfacing from the deep.

Liffey feared she might faint from the intense heat and mounting desperation she felt pounding in her chest. She obviously had not been breathing properly when she started escaping from this mamba.

'How fast could this snake travel?'

Liffey turned around and sprinted away again. She stopped, panting hard and looked back. The grass was still moving from approximately the same distance as the first time she had turned around to check.

The moving grass reminded Liffey of Max burrowing under shallow snow drifts in her Wisconsin back yard.

Liffey was beyond thirsty now. She knew she could not keep sprinting indefinitely and turning around like this to see if the mamba was still following her.

She was beginning to wear down.

The mamba was obviously keeping up with her.

It had to be traveling at least ten or twelve miles per hour. Liffey knew she would not be able to run at this pace for much longer in this heat.

She also knew that the black mamba would not quit.

This was mamba land. It was capable of following her for as long as it took.

It was only a matter of time before Liffey Rivers would be a dead American girl lying still in the tall savanna grasses in South Africa.

'Daddy is going to kill me for this,' Liffey thought as tears began to run down her face.

chapter 22

AUNT JEAN AND Mr. Powers finally managed to get their horses under control. Liffey's horse, Leonardo, had managed to stay with them while all three horses galloped wildly across the plain.

"We must be at least a mile away from Liffey, Mr. Powers!" Aunt Jean shouted.

"She might have already been eaten!"

"What am I supposed to say to my poor brother?"

"That I threw his precious little girl into a lions' den?"

"That I left her behind to be devoured?"

"Get a grip, Ms. Rivers," Mr. Powers commanded. "We need to get back to Liffey right now!"

Mr. Powers did not say what was really on his mind. That all three horses had been spooked and this never happened to horses like these unless they instinctively sensed mortal danger.

Like a poisonous snake ready to strike.

He was about to tell the Rivers ladies that the small hill with the flowering tree they were approaching looked like an abandoned termite mound when the horses had reared up and bolted.

He feared that it might already be too late for Liffey if that termite mound was inhabited by a black mamba. He should have led the horses away from the mound before they got so close. He knew that. His years as a Kruger Park ranger had taught him that. The colorful birds had distracted him.

"Now let's go get Liffey!"

He tied Leonardo to his horse and broke into a full gallop.

Jean Rivers would have to fend for herself for the time being. He had to get back to Liffey before it was too late.

✳ ✳ ✳

Sinead McGowan finally managed to finish her essay about endangered species in Ireland.

Writing legibly was becoming a real problem.

It seemed it was mostly birds that were vanishing at an alarming rate. It had to be because of the visiting birds like the cuach that Irish birds were becoming fewer and fewer.

The cuach lived mostly in Africa and turned up in Ireland each year in early spring to lay their eggs. She often heard one of them out in the fields just before first morning light calling, "cuckoo...cuckoo." It was always twice and faraway. She never actually saw one.

She signed and dated her paper. It was not due until after break but she would be in Wisconsin when school started up again. Her mother would deliver it to the school for her.

Tears began running down Sinead's face.

Cuckoos were terrible birds.

They would lay their evil cuckoo eggs in nests that already had Irish bird eggs in them waiting to hatch.

Then the baby cuckoos would hatch along with the other eggs in the nest. Somehow they were able to mimic the begging calls for food that the Irish hatchlings made.

Finally, when they had mooched enough food and become very strong, the baby cuckoos would push the non-cuckoo eggs and hatchlings out of the nest and the mother birds could not tell the cuckoos apart from their own baby birds.

Sinead began to talk to herself and sob inconsolably.

"This is just awful."

"Those poor little chicks are being pushed out of their own nests by those evil baby cuckoos!"

"And their mothers can't even tell the difference? What kind of mothers would not know that their own babies had been thrown to the ground and alien birds had invaded and taken over?"

Mrs. Theresa McGowan stood outside of Sinead's bedroom door alarmed. Sinead cried easily these days about everything and nothing.

The least little thing would set her off on an hour long crying binge.

'After she gets back from the States, I am taking her to Dr. Dorman. Maybe the doctor can figure out what is going on with her.'

'Something is just not right.'

chapter 23

THERE WAS A large tree directly ahead of Liffey but she knew that even if she could manage to climb it, the black mamba could easily follow her.

Liffey felt a familiar tightness in her chest. She had not had an asthma attack for months. If she had one now and passed out in this heat, it would be all over.

She *had* to get the upper hand here and get a hold of herself. This was, after all, *just* a snake. Not a man riding on a horse and aiming a gun at her in the fog on top of a mountain. She had been there and done that. *Surely* she could figure out how to escape from a snake!

'I can be faster than a snake.'

This thought gave her some much needed courage and she began to power walk, not run across the tall grass. This time she did not take the time to turn around to spot the mamba. She had to keep moving as fast as she could. And she needed to regulate her breathing more efficiently in the hot, dry air.

'How could this have happened? Where were Mr. Powers and Aunt Jean? She never expected anything much from her aunt, but where was the ranger with the gun?'

She could not resist one more look.

She must have slowed down when she was feeling sorry for herself because the snake was less than twenty feet behind her now, its head raised up high again above the tall grass. It was almost in striking range.

This snake was going to kill her.

This was going to be the end of Liffey Rivers.

She was going to die before she even got to know her mother again and her father would never, ever forgive her for going off on a dangerous expedition without him. With Aunt Jean of *all* people! He would never get over her stupidity.

The snake was going to sink its long fangs into her and she would die within the hour unless she stopped feeling sorry for herself.

'Not today. I am *not* going to die today from a stupid snake bite in the middle of a field in Africa.'

Liffey felt her feet begin to move again. She hardly noticed now how thirsty she was.

She felt light headed but that was fine. She needed to be light enough to fly. She was not sprinting. Now she was long distance running. 'It's a good thing I'm an Irish dancer,' she thought. 'Otherwise I would never be able to take this abuse.'

Memories of dancing on one hundred degree days at Irish Fest in Milwaukee flew through her head. Days when she was sure she would not last through her performances without collapsing. Somehow she always did make it through and she would get through this too.

She knew she would eventually have to turn around again to spot the snake and then pace herself accordingly. Now was as good a time as any. She spun around confidently. The snake was about fifty feet away again which was good. She had put more distance between them.

This was also bad because she was not sure how much longer she could keep moving like this, keeping her internal pep talk in sync with her stamina.

She was so thirsty she feared she might actually black out before the snake reached her.

She needed a miracle. There was still no sign of the horses or their riders. There was nowhere to run. This huge mamba could strike at her with deadly accuracy from five feet away.

"The black mamba is fast but I am *faster!*"

Liffey prayed for help.

Just as she was sure her lungs were going to burst out of her chest, the sky darkened like it had a few hours ago at the start of this ongoing nightmare journey to Camp Survival. The air cooled a bit and felt moist.

This time, sheets of water poured from the sky. Liffey wanted to stop and throw her head back and open her mouth to let the rain fill it up. Her clothes were soaked with the miracle cooling off rain and she was able to pick up her pace once again.

She turned around and saw that the mamba's head was no longer peeking above the grass line. The tall grasses were being flattened by the heavy rainfall.

'This has got to slow the snake down a bit,' she thought hopefully, licking rain water from her lips and running as fast as she could through the sloshing water which was beginning to turn the savanna grasses into a slimy marsh.

Not far ahead Liffey saw what looked like a fast moving stream. 'This heavy downpour must have filled up that riverbed in minutes,' she thought.

When Liffey got within a few feet of the torrential stream she could see that its current was deadly fast. Could there be crocodiles or hippos in this torrent of water? 'If I tried to jump over this water to escape from the snake and missed the other side, I might be throwing myself into a hippo's mouth downstream.'

Could a mamba swim or jump over such a fast moving stream?

She wondered if *she* could leap across this violently rushing water. The rain was pounding down so hard that the steep, muddy creek bank was turning into a mudslide.

The rain stopped and the sun roasted the earth again like an oven set at five hundred degrees. Steam rose from the soggy ground and the grasses started to spring up again.

She turned around quickly for another mamba check and groaned. This time, it was raised up again and moving towards her from no more than thirty feet away.

'How long have I been standing by this water spacing out? Too long it seems.'

The snake abruptly stopped and did a taunting half lunge.

"*Why* is this snake following me?" Liffey cried out desperately.

This was it.

She either pulled this off quickly or she died right here.

Nobody survived a black mamba bite out in the middle of nowhere unless they got antivenom within a very short time.

Aunt Jean had been gone for ages with Mr. Powers. 'Her waterproof mascara probably started running down her face in the rain and she's redoing her makeup,' Liffey thought bitterly.

Liffey reluctantly turned away from the snake even though she feared it might bite her in the neck from behind if she did not do something drastic within seconds.

She could not risk backing up for a running head start to propel herself across the rapids because then the mamba would ambush her from behind for sure. Somehow, she needed to leap over this water.

'*Leapover*!'

She would do a perfect Irish dance leapover. A sailing high, traveling far kind of leapover!

She would leap over this fast moving stream of water. It would be easy. She refused to think about what could happen if the perfect leapover did not work.

'I can fly,' thought Liffey, getting up on her toes as best she could in the soggy grass. She did two little skips and launched herself across the water.

At her highest soaring point, she felt something tugging on the bottom of her right snake boot, like there was a weight attached to her foot. For an instant she feared she had caught her foot on a floating tree branch and would be dragged downstream after all.

In spite of the additional weight, Liffey managed to get to the other side of the stream safely, faltering a bit as she landed.

Before she could get her bearings again, she felt a crunching sensation under her right foot and something at least eight feet long whipped by her at ground level and began thrashing around on the grass. In a few seconds it stopped and lay still.

The black mamba's fangs were embedded in the sole of her right boot. The expensive snake boots that Aunt Jean had insisted they purchase for this safari had saved her life because the soles of the boots were reinforced with steel plates.

Liffey was stunned. She could not help thinking about Dorothy's house landing on the Wicked Witch of the East and the witch's ruby slippers sticking out from underneath.

Liffey could not decide whether she was about to become hysterical or throw up, or both, when she heard a high pitched voice screaming:

"Liffey! Liffey! You are alive!"

chapter 24

ROBERT RIVERS HAD begun to feel like he was living on the other side of the veil. Maeve's in between earth and dream talking tangents were beginning to exhaust him. He needed to get his wife back to Wisconsin to set up some kind of normal routine and had already hired a full time nurse to live in the small guest house next to the gate.

Nurse Sheila Sullivan would be responsible for Maeve's physical and medical needs. He and Liffey would provide mental stimulation and if worse came to worse, his sister Jean could spell them.

Maeve still had friends in Chicago who did not know she had reappeared. Maybe they could come up from time to time and help jog her memory. He stroked Maeve's forehead. Her eyes were open but she was not fully awake when she started to speak in an agitated voice:

"Push off hard from your toes, Liffey. I know you can do it. You can fly over the water if you try! You must do it now, Liffey. No time to think. Just do it!" At least this mysterious ranting was in English. Maeve is probably remembering a game she used to play with Liffey,' Robert Rivers thought.

"That reminds me, Maeve, I will call Liffey soon and let her know everything is in place."

✳ ✳ ✳

Neil had made up his mind he was never practicing his violin again after the Johannesburg feis was over. He had practiced enough for the rest of his life. Sister Helen was always snooping in the hallway, listening. It was like it was a matter of life and death or something.

✳ ✳ ✳

Mr. Powers dismounted and cocked his rifle, aiming carefully at Liffey's right foot. Even though the black mamba attached to Liffey's boot was not moving, he was treating this as a dangerous situation.

"Liffey, do not move. It appears the snake is dead but it might just be stunned. Even if the snake is dead, there is still the possibility that its fangs are deep in the boot near your bare foot and venom could seep into a little scratch or blister you might not even know you have on your foot."

"We need to be extremely cautious taking off your boot. First, I will remove the snake. Then we will check the boot for fang punctures."

"Mr. Powers, I am positive this snake is dead and that its fangs have not penetrated my boot. My boots have steel reinforcements above their rubber soles. Aunt Jean decided to buy these snake boots after the cobra got into our living room. The mamba must have struck at me from behind just as I started my leap over the stream."

Mr. Powers looked a bit confused and said: "There was a cobra in your house?"

Before Liffey could explain, Mr. Powers asked Liffey to sit on the ground so he could pull the snake from her boot. He detached the snake's head, stretched it out full length and said: "This mamba is over eight feet long, Liffey. I don't know how you managed to jump across the creek with it attached to your boot."

"I didn't jump, Mr. Powers. I did a leapover."

"A *what* over?"

"A leapover. It's an Irish dance step that gets you airborne if you do it properly. The mamba must have struck at me just when I tucked my right leg under me and pointed my foot backwards."

Mr. Powers looked very confused. "How could you leap if your leg was tucked under you with your foot pointed backwards?"

Liffey started to explain but decide it was too hard to describe to someone if they were not an Irish dancer.

"I will show you a leapover at the camp."

"So you *danced* across this water with a black mamba snake attached to your foot?"

"I guess you could put it that way. But I did not know it was a snake until I landed on the other side. It looked more like a loose jump rope attached to my foot."

"Well, I guess I've seen everything now, Ms. Rivers."

"Just hang around me for awhile, Mr. Powers. This kind of thing is pretty normal."

After the ranger had carefully pulled off Liffey's boot and placed the snake twenty feet away from where Liffey sat, he turned it over with the snake hook he had retrieved from his backpack.

"No doubt, this mamba is definitely a goner, Liffey. These mambas have bones in their mouths that push their fangs out and down when the snake strikes. When the mamba struck the heavy tread on the bottom of your boot, its fangs became embedded in the sole."

"Did the snake come at you near the termite mound after the horses got spooked?"

After Liffey explained what had happened, Mr. Powers shook his head incredulously.

"Would you like me to skin the snake for you, Ms. Rivers, for a souvenir?"

Aunt Jean, who had been crouching nearby watching and listening, suddenly stood up and shuddered. She began to raise her arm in protest but heaved a great sigh instead. She seemed to be speechless.

"No thanks, Mr. Powers. I only want to remember this black mamba incident when I need to get really good lift for a leapover."

"All right then, let's get your aunt back up on her horse and get out of here."

Liffey did not talk as she slowly walked over to greet Leo, her runaway horse.

Mr. Powers broke the silence. "I apologize for the erratic behavior of the horses, Liffey. They sensed the mamba and were terrified. Horses seem to know when their lives are in danger and a mamba has more than enough venom to kill a horse."

"Mambas strike repeatedly when they get agitated. I've heard up to twelve times."

✳ ✳ ✳

Sister Helen was worried about Neil. Instead of being excited about his first paying job as a musician in a few more days, he seemed preoccupied and nervous.

It was almost as if he had a sense of foreboding about something.

One thing was certain. He did not want to discuss whatever it was that was bothering him with her.

He was respectful and polite but she could tell that he was determined not to bat the breeze with her anytime soon.

Until he came around and told her what it was that was bothering him, all she could do was continue praying to Saint Patrick to watch over and protect him.

Lately she had boldly suggested that the saint put in a good word with his Boss concerning the restoration of Neil's leg muscles.

Sister Helen believed in miracles.

chapter 25

AT FIRST, AUNT Jean refused to get back up on her horse.

"Surely you cannot be serious, Mr. Powers? I simply do not have the strength to endure any more disasters today. I am afraid you will have to send for help. I suggest a helicopter."

Mr. Powers looked surprised. Liffey could tell he was trying to think of something diplomatic to say to Aunt Jean.

'He might totally blow our whole safari if he says something sensible that really freaks her out like, "There are no helicopters available out here unless it's an emergency."'

'This one's up to me,' Liffey thought apprehensively.

After Liffey convinced her aunt there were probably more snakes in the vicinity and that they did not want to be hanging around here like sitting ducks waiting for a helicopter, Aunt Jean agreed and mounted her horse.

Mr. Powers shook his head and gave Liffey a friendly thank you smile.

"All right then ladies, we're off. If we are lucky, we will still make it to base camp in time for a dinner of boerewors on braai and carrot achaar."

"Whatever is he talking about Liffey?"

"Remember how you told me on the plane that we were going to a foreign country and that things were going to be different, Aunt Jean? Well we are in a foreign country now and things are definitely different here."

To Liffey's surprise, Aunt Jean nodded wisely and told her Boerperd horse to "giddy up."

✳ ✳ ✳

The sun was brutal. Even hotter than Liffey had imagined it could ever be. Every half hour they stopped to let the horses drink from the fast moving stream they were following to the camp.

After they had been riding for a few hours, thick vegetation appeared on the horizon. The stream had widened and deepened and there were high leadwood trees lining its banks.

"Is this a mirage, Mr. Powers, or are we going to get some heat relief soon?"

"About twenty more minutes, Liffey. We'll be there in twenty minutes. Keep your eyes open and you will probably see a hippo or two."

"We will no longer be splashing ourselves with stream water from this point on because the hippos contaminate the rest of the downstream water. Keep your eyes open. They are very aggressive, dangerous animals."

"If we were to dismount here and lead our horses to the river, we could lose our heads. Hippos often decapitate their victims. Up until now, the moving water has kept their manky waste moving downstream and away from us. But now you can see that the banks have become reedy and the water is becoming stagnant. This stream is headed for a small lake."

"Right before we reach the lake, we will be turning west and moving in the opposite direction."

Liffey glanced nervously behind her.

'Thank goodness Aunt Jean is listening to her music again. If she had heard what Mr. Powers just said about hippos decapitating people, we would be so back in Johannesburg tomorrow.'

Mr. Powers' prediction of a hippo sighting did not take long.

A large hippopotamus surfaced near the shore about thirty yards away and yawned. Liffey grabbed her camcorder.

"More people are killed in Africa by hippos than any other animals, ladies. That yawn is not about being sleepy. It's a sign of aggression. Follow me," Mr. Powers ordered, reining his horse sharply left and away from the water.

Liffey asked, "Why then, if they are so dangerous, aren't hippos on the Big Five list, Mr. Powers?"

"Good question. The Big Five list was created long ago by big game hunters when safaris in Africa were mostly about bagging a big trophy animal. They were the animals hunters most wanted to shoot. These days, safaris are mostly about shooting animals with cameras instead of guns."

"Hippos are on the Dangerous Six list. They can run at eighteen miles per hour so outrunning them is out of the question unless you are on horseback."

"By the way, if we pass a rhino it is also high alert time. Rhinos will charge unprovoked. The good thing is that they have very poor eyesight. They will smell you long before they see you. When we are walking on trails, it is best to get behind a tree if one charges."

"Since hippos live next to water, this will probably be our only sighting until we are returning to the jeep in a few days. With some luck we should be spotting some rhinos pretty soon."

Liffey had mixed feelings about spotting anymore animals. She had already almost been killed by a black mamba before she even got close to camp.

One near-death experience per day was enough.

'Maybe this safari was not such a great idea after all.'

chapter 26

LIFFEY SAW IT first.

A high observation deck with a wooden tower above the trees.

Camp Survival, at last!

It was almost noon and she was famished. She could not wait to eat whatever it was Mr. Powers thought the cook might be preparing and then plop down on a cot in her tent. She hoped that Aunt Jean would be too exhausted to notice that they were not at a luxury hotel with spas and waiters.

❋ ❋ ❋

When they rode into camp, Liffey saw eight small tents set up under a canopy of what Mr. Powers said were knobthorn trees.

Flames were rising from an outdoor oven in a small clearing and a pleasant looking white haired man dressed in khaki was putting what looked like sausages on the grill.

"Hello my little noo noos!" he called out cheerfully.

"Noo noos?" asked Liffey.

Aunt Jean said, "He is speaking French to us Liffey. How exciting! This is very continental."

"I don't think he means 'nous' like in French, Aunt Jean." Liffey had taken a six week summer school course in French at Fish Creek Elementary School when she was ten. "I think 'nous' in French means 'we.' Why would he say, 'Hello my little we wees?'"

"Whatever," Aunt Jean replied. "It is obvious that man is very polished. He has an interesting accent."

"I think it is a Dutch accent, Aunt Jean."

"Perhaps, Liffey. We must freshen up in our room and then present ourselves properly."

"Present ourselves, Aunt Jean?"

"Yes, Liffey, in polite society one must present oneself."

"O.K. We will present ourselves, Aunt Jean, as soon as we freshen up."

❈ ❈ ❈

Aunt Jean screeched when she saw a giant snail as big as her fist outside the entrance to their tent.

"Liffey! Get it! Get it out of here immediately! Call Mr. Powers!"

"Aunt Jean, it's only a big snail. It can't harm us."

"I know very well it would not wish to hurt us, Liffey. I just do not want to look at it. It's hideous."

Liffey was surprised that Aunt Jean had apparently not noticed yet that they were going to be sleeping in a very small tent with only one table between their cots.

"If that snail creature managed to get past camp security and almost into our tent, heaven only knows what else is lurking outside planning and plotting to do the same thing."

"We must keep one eye open when we sleep at night, Liffey."

chapter 27

WHEN AUNT JEAN found out that the way to take a shower at camp was to take a large plastic bag, fill it up with cold water, hang it on a tree branch, turn it upside down and then aim the nozzle down, she wanted to leave immediately.

No hot water.

No laundry service.

No gourmet meals.

No special attention of any kind.

A tent.

A cot.

A giant snail.

Liffey persuaded her aunt to at least spend the night, just in case things turned out to be interesting the next day after all.

✳ ✳ ✳

Liffey woke up the next morning to the sound of neighing horses and distant conversation. The sun was beginning to leak in through the canvas tent walls and Aunt Jean was snoring on her cot. The early morning air smelled fresh and full of possibilities.

Yesterday, after Liffey and her aunt had dined on the delicious farmers sausages and the carrot dish Colonel Peterson had prepared, they both fell fast asleep on their cots long before sunset.

"Nervous exhaustion," is what Mr. Powers told Colonel Peterson the Rivers were suffering from. After hearing the story of the runaway horses and the black mamba following Liffey and latching on to her foot, Colonel Peterson agreed they must be completely frazzled. He made them a cup of what he called 'safari snooze' tea and sent them to bed.

❋ ❋ ❋

Mr. Powers opened the tent door flap and announced that breakfast was ready and that they would be leaving in forty-five minutes for their first day of big game tracking.

Liffey was surprised when Aunt Jean eagerly got up and announced she would hurry ahead of Liffey and meet her later in the dining tent.

Aunt Jean was always unpredictable.

After Liffey had carefully packed her mini backpack for her first day of tracking the Big Ten, she carefully zipped the tent door shut to keep out bugs and snails and headed over to the dining area.

Aunt Jean was sitting at a picnic table with a mug of coffee, propping her chin up with her hands on the table and flirting big time with Colonel Peterson. Mr. Powers had told them that Colonel Peterson was a retired army officer. Aunt Jean had learned he was also a bachelor. 'This is great,' thought Liffey. 'Aunt Jean will want to impress Colonel Peterson and won't want to show him what a wimp she is.'

"Good morning, everybody!" Liffey said enthusiastically, "Happy Christmas!"

"I think you mean 'Merry Christmas,' Liffey, darling."

Liffey did not correct her aunt and tell her that people in this part of the world usually said 'happy' not 'merry' Christmas.

'Everybody' was Aunt Jean, Colonel Peterson, Mr. Powers and two middle-aged stern looking women who clearly disapproved of Aunt Jean's flirting so obviously.

Aunt Jean was oblivious to the women's critical looks while Colonel Peterson told her about a trip down the Nile River he had taken a million years ago looking for rare crocodiles.

Liffey turned to Colonel Peterson. "Colonel Peterson, what do we need to know before we start off this morning?"

The colonel took the hint and announced to the entire table that it was time to set out on their trek.

"Your attention please, ladies! A few pointers before we begin our first day of tracking the Big Five and the Dangerous Six."

"Do any of you know which animals belong to these groups?"

Liffey expected Aunt Jean to chime in because they had gone over the Big Five list at least a hundred times, but she did not. She just sat there with her chin cupped in her hands trying to look dumb.

The other two ladies did not seem to know so Liffey spoke up: "The Big Five animals are the Lion, Cape Buffalo, Rhinoceros, Leopard and Elephant. The Dangerous Six is made up of all of the Big Five animals but also includes the Hippopotamus."

"Well done, young lady! Now, can you tell me which rhino is in these groupings?"

"Pardon, me, Colonel, but I don't know what you mean," Liffey answered.

To Liffey's complete astonishment, Aunt Jean spoke up: "It would be the Black Rhino, not the White Rhino, Colonel." She smiled demurely.

"Amazing, after years of trekking with groups here in the bush, only a handful of people have known that there are both black and white rhinos."

Aunt Jean smiled smugly at the rigid women who said their names were Gertrude and Alice.

"It is highly unlikely we will see a black rhino but the odds of spotting a white rhino are very good. The rhino has three distinct toes which we will look for on the trails."

"Does anyone know what a group of rhinos is called?" Colonel Peterson looked around the group smiling. Then he closed his eyes while he waited for answers.

Again, it was Aunt Jean who chimed in after a short pause. "A herd of rhinos normally has approximately 14 members, and is called a 'crash of rhinos,' Colonel."

Liffey was amazed. Could it be that she had never noticed before that her Aunt Jean was some kind of weird genius? 'That's impossible. Aunt Jean's brain is a vacant lot. I don't know how she is pulling this off.'

Then it hit her. Aunt Jean had her mobile phone on her lap! She was online googling for answers while Gertrude and Alice were discussing the questions with their heads together in earnest, hushed tones.

✳ ✳ ✳

The small trekking group had only been walking for a short time when Colonel Peterson stopped them and pointed to the long scrape marks underneath their feet on the trail. Like something sharp had scratched lines into the dirt.

"These are rhino horn scrapings, ladies. If you look a few feet ahead, you will see four perfect three-toe foot imprints. We are officially tracking one of the Big Five now." Mr. Powers, bringing up the rear, began loading his rifle chamber with bullets. The Colonel wore his big automatic hand gun on a belt.

"How can you tell if we are tracking a black rhino or a white one, Colonel?" Liffey asked.

"Good question, Liffey. White rhinos travel with their crashes. The black rhino tends to be solitary. We have tracks here for one rhino only so the odds are it is a black rhino, which is as you know, one of the Big Five."

Liffey's heart rate picked up. A shivery thrill ran through her. When the mamba had chased her yesterday, she had been on the defensive, fleeing in terror for her life. Today, *she* was the tracker. She was stalking one of the Big Five!

"Rhinos do a lot of eating, ladies. They spend half of each day feeding on grass. Males weigh around five thousand pounds and females around three thousand eight hundred. If they can find a mud hole, they will wallow in it most of the day to keep cool."

"My experience with the rhinos around here is that they will come down this trail on the way to the mud hole a short way ahead of us which fills up with rain from time to time. It rained heavily yesterday so it is likely we will find a few of these beasts today at their spa cooling off."

Colonel Peterson wiped his brow. It was already beginning to get very hot in the early morning sun.

"An interesting fact about white rhinos is that they are not white. They are grey. The word for 'wide' in Dutch sounds like the word 'white' in English and that's how they got their name. And black rhinos are also grey. What could make more sense?"

Colonel Peterson suddenly stopped talking and raised his arm and made a fist.

Liffey was scarcely breathing. She knew a rhino had to be directly in front of them, probably heading for the mud hole or maybe already in it.

A loud bellowing noise penetrated the silence and then there were pounding feet moving directly towards them on the trail.

Mr. Powers pulled Aunt Jean, who was walking directly behind Liffey with her trekking poles, off the trail and behind a tree with him and directed Liffey to a large nearby tree trunk.

Colonel Peterson reminded everyone else to quickly take cover. "The rhino smelled us and is charging," he said calmly. He removed his gun from its holster.

Gertrude and Alice huddled together behind the thick trunk of a dead tree. Colonel Peterson found a sizable rock and lowered himself to the ground behind it.

Liffey stood immobile. Her feet seemed to have forgotten how to move her body towards the safety of the large leadwood tree trunk Mr. Powers had pointed out.

She was not afraid. She was fascinated by the rhythm of the rhino's feet hitting the ground like sledge hammers and the loud howling roar it was making like a train engine's whistle.

She knew she needed to move, it was just that her feet would not budge.

When Liffey saw the rhino coming right at her at what seemed like the speed of light, she raced to the tree trunk and quickly jumped behind it.

The rhino roared as it ran by her and then came to a complete halt.

Liffey knew it had poor eyesight and could probably would not see her if it turned around. But she also knew it had acute hearing and its smelling cavities were bigger than its brain.

Everyone shifted their positions to the other side of their protective trees and rocks in case the rhino reversed direction and came back at them again.

She heard Mr. Powers cock his rifle.

She did not want this poor rhino to die.

She would be happy to hide behind the tree all day until it went away.

She could tell it was a black rhino as it ran by her because it did not have a wide square mouth with huge lips. It had elongated, pointy lips.

It occurred to Liffey that she had now seen all of the Big Five and the Dangerous Six!

The rhino, which was completely covered in mud, did not turn around. It snorted and walked away from the relieved trekkers.

chapter 28

"IT'S TIME FOR a siesta," Colonel Peterson announced as the expedition regrouped off the trail in a thicket of jackleberry trees.

He reached into his oversized backpack and gave each trekker a lightweight hammock.

"Now find yourself a place to hang your hammock, ladies. After you eat your bagged lunches, we will nap for one hour and then find the local zebra dazzle. I caught a whiff of fresh zebra dung a mile back. They are definitely grazing nearby."

✳ ✳ ✳

Aunt Jean made a serious mistake while she was lounging in her hammock. She texted her brother Robert Rivers:

"U will never believe what just happened! We narrowly escaped with our lives a few minutes ago when a black rhino charged us! After Liffey's narrow escape yesterday with the black mamba, it was almost too much for us to cope with! Heaven only knows what lies ahead tonight. Will have a lovely Christmas feast prepared by a charming army officer. Merry Christmas brother, darling. My best to Maeve. Love-J."

✳ ✳ ✳

Attorney Rivers was eating a Christmas dinner of turkey, ham, vegetables and pudding with his wife in her hospital room when his message alert beep went off. Maeve was in good spirits. She knew that it was Christmas Day. She was sitting up in bed and feeding herself. She was smiling.

Robert Rivers read his text message and immediately dialed Sam Snyder's cell phone. He did not care that it was Christmas Day. He was furious. How dare Snyder allow his sister and Liffey to place themselves in mortal danger without his consent? He was well aware that Snyder and his other staff detectives did not share his concern that 'the skunk man,' as Liffey called him, was not dead and still very much a threat to his daughter and wife.

Still, he expected Sam and the other detectives on his staff to monitor Liffey's movements and protect her.

Sam *had* told him that Jean and Liffey had gone to the Liberty Torch Feis in New York, but he had omitted the small detail that they had not returned to the Milwaukee Airport afterwards.

Instead, they had flown from New York to AFRICA! And not only to Africa, they went on a safari and Liffey had apparently almost been killed twice within the last twenty-four hours! And his sister apparently thought this was all very exciting! Mr. Snyder had better have a very good explanation for this disaster.

✳ ✳ ✳

Just as Liffey was drifting asleep in her comfortable hammock, Aunt Jean's phone rang. 'I bet that it's Daddy calling to wish us a Merry Christmas,' Liffey thought happily.

'He beat me to it.'

chapter 29

"LIFFEY DARLING, I am afraid I have bad news."

"We must leave Camp Serenity tomorrow morning."

"Somehow your father found out that we are here on safari and for some reason he thinks we are in danger."

"He is furious with me for not disclosing our trip."

"I tried to explain to him that we are doing an important science unit for my School of Life course but that explanation seemed to make him even more furious."

"I finally gave into the unreasonable pressure he was exerting and agreed to be airlifted by helicopter tomorrow morning at 8:00 a.m. to Johannesburg, with you, of course. Apparently, Mr. Powers will accompany us."

Liffey was devastated.

This was only the second day of being on a real safari.

How had her father found out where they were?

She had never lied to him when they spoke or texted.

She had just never mentioned that they happened to be in Africa.

At Camp Ukuthula, it had hardly mattered. That place was about as dangerous as a Rain Forest Café.

She knew Sinead would not have betrayed her confidence.

She also knew Sinead would not have lied to her father either if he had asked her where she was for some good reason.

Sinead simply would not have brought the subject up.

'It isn't like I've run off with a stranger,' Liffey thought. 'I'm with his *sister*.'

"The good thing about having to get back to Jo'berg," Aunt Jean finished, "is that now we will be able to practice properly for the feis at our hotel. And we will be able to shop and get a facial."

"Also, I have to admit that I have not been pointing my toes properly while walking on the trails, Liffey, have you?"

chapter 30

THERE WERE TEARS in Aunt Jean's eyes that night after a sumptuous Christmas supper when Colonel Peterson took her hand and kissed it like some kind of ancient movie star and told her that the Zulu words for saying goodbye if you are leaving a place are, "Sulani Kahle."

On the table there was a small branch decorated with red and gold Christmas ornaments and individual paper crowns to wear. Each plate had a Christmas cracker placed in front of it. After an excellent pudding, which Liffey suspected contained a major overdose of whiskey, everyone put on the little paper party crowns.

The cracker tugging began and when the crackers popped open, little silver safari animal charms flew all over the table.

It was hard to be sure which charms had been in each of the individual crackers so Liffey grabbed a silver snake charm that had landed in front of Gertrude without asking first. "I really, really deserve this snake charm," she explained to Alice and Gertrude who were visibly shocked by her poor manners.

✳ ✳ ✳

After supper, Liffey asked permission to spend some time on the viewing deck since she and Aunt Jean were leaving in the morning.

Although Liffey was anxious to practice her dance steps at the hotel in Johannesburg, she was not so anxious that she wanted to leave this safari after only two days. Especially since so much of the first day was spent fleeing from the black mamba.

✳ ✳ ✳

Liffey climbed up the stairs to the fifty-foot-high viewing deck wearing her Irish dance hard shoes. She also carried her camcorder since it had night vision capability.

The wooden deck would be a perfect place to practice her treble jig and hornpipe until it got too dark to be safe. 'There is no way I am risking twisting my ankle in the dark after all I have been through lately,' Liffey thought.

It was nice being in Africa on safari on Christmas Day. It was odd not going to church and singing Christmas carols but being in the middle of nowhere with wild animals strolling about like people in a shopping mall gave Christmas a whole new feeling.

Her favorite Christmas theme had always been the one where the lion and lamb would one day live together peacefully, led by a little child.

✳ ✳ ✳

The sky finally darkened after a beautiful orange and red sunset. Mr. Powers had joined Liffey briefly to instruct her that he was going to accompany her back to her tent when she had finished viewing nocturnal animals from the deck.

"Here's a whistle, Liffey. Blow on it twice and I will come right up and get you to escort you back to your tent."

"Blow on it three times if you have any problems or concerns up here."

"Remember, you are not to return to your tent unaccompanied. It's a camp rule. Curfew is 10:00 p.m."

"Also, please knock off the tap dancing soon."

"People are trying to sleep and it sounds like there is a herd of stampeding elephants running around up here."

❊ ❊ ❊

Except for the brilliant stars shining above the trees, it was pitch black. There was no moon in the sky.

The Christmas bonfire had been extinguished.

Except for crickets, there were no sounds interrupting the absolute silence.

With her night seeing camcorder, Liffey could make out a group of what appeared to be baboons peacefully sleeping in the tree branches below.

When she looked east, she thought she saw a leopard stalking an antelope but they were too far away to tell for sure.

The moon rose, filtering its light in the tree branches below. She could now see that something was moving towards the camp from the north. From a distance Liffey estimated to be about the length of a football field, she thought she saw a group of large cats creeping towards the camp.

They were moving along stealthily like they were stalking something. Two big cats were out in front leading the others.

Liffey watched closely hoping they had not spotted a baby buffalo or giraffe sleeping away from its mother's watch. She was studying the area between herself and the cats carefully but she could see no sign of any prey animal.

Maybe they were going to attack the sleeping baboons below her? If so, this was going to be too close for comfort. She felt for the whistle on the cord around her neck.

The cats moved forward.

Then stopped.

Moved forward.

Then stopped.

Liffey could see them more clearly now. As she had suspected, the large cats were lions and there were at least ten of them.

The lions kept advancing. They crept past the trees with the sleeping baboons. They were closing in on something.

Liffey saw another pride of lions approaching from the east. There did not seem to be anything territorial going on. Both prides were creeping along in unison like a chorus line.

When the lions reached the clearing just before the camp boundary, they split up and began to circle the camp.

This looked very bad.

Flashes of the man-eating lion movie erupted in Liffey's head.

Was this really happening? Was Aunt Jean going to be taken from her tent and eaten tonight? Were these man-eating lions?

Maybe her aunt was not crazy? Maybe she was psychic!

Liffey grabbed the whistle around her neck but decided that might not be wise. The lions seemed to be in no rush. She needed to watch closely before she sounded the alarm.

Ever since the incident in St. Louis with the Irish dancer doll, Liffey had become accustomed to being thrown completely off balance with little or no warning and this had given her an edge most people never developed.

She was amazed how level-headed she felt now watching these huge lions stalking the camp. This was just another ordinary day. It had only been a few hours since the last deadly animal had tried to kill her. She was starting to get used to this survival game.

At Camp Ukuthula, Liffey remembered she had talked with Mr. Powers on his mobile phone before he had picked them up at the elephant reserve. She needed to call him now and warn him not to come out of his tent. She found his number, pressed redial and waited.

One ring.

Two rings.

Three rings. 'He is not going to answer.'

She was about to hang up and blow the large whistle three times when she heard a sleepy, "Hello?"

"Mr. Powers, this is Liffey Rivers from up on the deck. There are at least twenty lions circling our camp. What should we do?"

"Twenty lions?" he asked incredulously. "Is this a joke, Liffey?"

"I'm afraid not. There may even be more than twenty, Mr. Powers. They are behaving like they are stalking something but nothing is out there that I can see."

"Dear Lord!" he exclaimed. "Stay put Liffey and whatever you do, do not move. I will call for help. I have never heard of anything like this before."

The line went dead.

'This is so unfair, everybody's sleeping.'

Liffey tried hard not to think about the man-eating lions of Tsavo.

'Everybody is trapped in their tents. Mr. Powers can get some help eventually but it might be too late by the time it arrives. I need to do something right now.'

The lions were now crouching in the same advance attack formation she had seen the other lions take when they were waiting to pounce on the baby buffalo crossing the road. Time was running out. Somebody had to do something.

Liffey crept slowly to the tower room to see if any of its contents might help. She found a huge spotlight in the middle of the room for nocturnal animal spotting. If there was any luck to be had here, it would be that the batteries in it were not dead.

'Lions would probably hate a harsh white light aimed at them.' The roof of the tower room was some kind of thin metal like tin. 'I can pound on the roof after I turn the spotlight on them.'

Liffey lifted the heavy light and managed to get it out on the deck and then up on to a wide ledge. She took a deep breath and pressed the switch. It was even better than she had hoped! The light from it was blinding. She moved the beam smoothly, sweeping over the ground from left to right, from lion to lion, like a spotlight at a movie premiere. The bright light bathed an area of at least fifty feet.

Liffey could see that the lions were becoming disoriented. She ran back into the tower room and looked in the corners for a broom handle or some kind of long stick. She found a filthy mop handle and began banging on the tin roof. The ringing noise was deafening.

'This might actually work,' she thought hopefully.

She blew her whistle in short bursts while she treble jigged over to the boom box on the deck that Colonel Peterson had given her to play Christmas carols.

Loud rap music played instead which perfectly suited her noise-making plan.

She turned the volume up as high as the dial would go and began doing her hornpipe, pounding her feet on the wooden deck as hard as she could.

Liffey had been making out-of-control noise for almost three minutes when she heard a shrill voice screaming through the din:

"Liffey, darling! Liffey! Liffey! Please tell me you are alive! Are you alive?"

Aunt Jean was followed by a breathless Gertrude and panting Alice. Colonel Peterson was only a few steps behind. He immediately leaned over the deck and coolly began shooting blank bullets at the lions which had begun to slink back into the darkness.

There was no sign of Mr. Powers.

chapter 31

WHEN ROBERT RIVERS asked Sinead if she had known all along that Liffey was in Africa with her Aunt Jean, Sinead burst into tears.

"I am so sorry, Mr. Rivers. Liffey asked me not to mention it to you but also said that if you ever asked, I could not lie to you about it."

The crying got worse.

Right now little baby birds were probably being pushed out of their nests by baby cuckoos. No. Not now. Not yet. Birds lay their eggs in the spring. Not at Christmas. Baby birds were not murdered at Christmas.

"Sinead, I am not accusing you of doing anything wrong. Believe me, I know how Liffey operates."

"She is often guilty of sins of omission. She knows very well what she should or should not tell me."

"She often chooses to ignore minor little details like going on a dangerous safari with my sister or finding missing mothers on mountain tops."

"I talk to or text her everyday and until I received a text from Jean about a rhino charging at them and a black mamba almost biting Liffey, I thought they were back in Wisconsin after a feis they went to in New York."

"My staff knew where they were and had arranged protection in South Africa but I was left completely out of the loop here in Ireland."

"I know everyone's intentions were good. I am here with Liffey's mother in a very delicate situation."

"But for heaven's sake! What kind of aunt takes her brother's child to Africa of all places on a safari and doesn't bother mentioning it to him until someone is almost killed!"

Attorney Rivers continued his ranting and that was fine with Sinead. Let him vent. Her head was hurting again. She could not stop thinking about all those poor little birds that would die this spring when the cuckoos flew to Ireland from Africa.

Mr. Rivers was right. Africa was a very, very dangerous place.

"My guess is that Jean never intended to tell me where they had gone and after things got rough, with snakes and rhinos and only God knows what else, she decided to boogie out of there and get back to the good life in five star hotels with beauty parlors and room service and boutiques."

"School of Life! What a joke!"

Robert Rivers took a deep breath. "Are you packed Sinead? Please stop crying. I am not angry with you for not telling me Liffey was in Africa. You wanted to spare me the worry. Maybe you can straighten Liffey out. Please stop crying. None of this is your fault. We leave for Wisconsin in just three more days."

Black Mamba!

The words felt like a knife had stabbed him in the head. Maeve had been repeatedly warning both of them about a mamba that might harm Liffey but until right now he had no idea what she had meant.

That threat was over.

chapter 32

BLACK MAMBA'S GOOD life continued in its comfortable cage.

Good food.

Plenty of water.

Hot but not too hot.

Life was easy.

✳ ✳ ✳

The motionless black mamba next to the stream had been collected by a graduate student from Wales doing field research. Perhaps its venom could be extracted and used for a batch of antivenom. He wondered how this snake had died. Its head was flattened like something had stepped on it.

✳ ✳ ✳

Sister Helen was holding Neil Roberts' left hand. He was pale and unresponsive with IV bags plugged into his thin right arm. "We have done everything we can, Sister. It's up to him now. If you have any special prayers, this would be a good time to say them. There will be a turning point for him soon. Either way…"

Sister Helen shot up in bed like a cannon ball. She looked fearfully around her sparsely furnished bedroom. She was not in a hospital room holding little Neil's hand. She had been dreaming. "Blessed be to God and His angels and His saints." She took in a deep breath and was asleep again before her head hit the pillow.

✳ ✳ ✳

"Where is Mr. Powers?" Liffey asked fearfully.

"Is he all right?" Liffey caught the look of disapproval Gertrude and Alice fired directly at Aunt Jean.

"What is it, Aunt Jean? Do you know what happened to Mr. Powers?"

"She most certainly does, young lady. Your aunt has probably killed the poor man! It remains to be seen yet whether or not she will have killed the rest of us as well! She extended an invitation to all the lions in South Africa to come to our camp tonight for a pig roast!"

"What?" Liffey was incredulous. She could not imagine anything Aunt Jean could do that would not be entirely harmless. Stupid, yes, but not harmful.

Aunt Jean tried to explain.

"After the snake and rhino attacks, I decided that we all needed more protection so I activated my warthog scent candle right outside our tent. Warthogs are such ugly creatures that I thought their smell would keep dangerous beasts like lions far away from us."

Liffey groaned and said, "I meant to ask you what the warthog scent was for on your list of things to bring, Aunt Jean, but I forgot."

Gertrude shook her head in disgust. "Who in their right mind would set off a lion lure in the middle of a camp?"

Alice chimed in. "So poor Mr. Powers went off to de-activate the warthog candle or whatever it is your aunt set off. It will be a miracle if he makes it back up here alive."

Colonel Peterson interrupted.

"Ladies there is no need to blame poor Jean here."

"She had the best of intentions and I do believe Liffey has cleverly managed to frighten the lions away for the time being."

"Lions are poor climbers. If they do mount an attack up the stairs, we can repel it I am sure."

"But I doubt very much that we will see any more of them tonight. They have been exposed to loud rap music and the thunderous noise from Liffey's tap dancing feet and I am sure they will now want to slink back to their lairs and recover their hearing."

"Excuse me for interrupting, Colonel. But we Irish dancers call it 'hard shoe,' not 'tap dancing.'"

"I see," said Colonel Peterson. "Thank you for so timely pointing that out, Jean."

Colonel Peterson went on. "When Mr. Powers arrives we..."

"Ladies," a familiar man's voice shouted from the bottom of the stairs, "we are lion free!"

Mr. Powers began walking up the platform stairs, apparently unharmed. "Did you see the small plane that flew over our camp a few minutes ago? They radioed me that they spotted two large groups of lions literally running away from us."

"I think we have our youngest group member to thank for that. She intuitively knew that if she made enough of a din, the lions might think twice about coming any closer."

"I have buried the warthog scent dispenser in a steel container so there will be no more olfactory dinner invitations wafting through the air tonight."

"Now, let us all get some much needed rest."

chapter 33

COLONEL PETERSON TOOK Aunt Jean's hand again and kissed it.

He said farewell in English this time and promised he would keep in touch.

Aunt Jean sighed and told the Colonel she would always remember the few magical days she spent at Camp Serenity.

The Colonel looked somewhat confused and said, "As will I, my dear."

Gertrude and Alice did not come out of their tent to say good-bye. Liffey strongly suspected that both of them were related to Principal Godzilla.

Mr. Powers carried all three backpacks to the clearing where they were to wait for the helicopter ride to Johannesburg.

Aunt Jean tried to hide the relief she felt now that they were leaving.

Liffey did not want to leave but at least she had seen all of the Big Five and then some.

Aunt Jean told her she was going to give her an 'A' for this School of Life science unit.

Liffey wanted to tell her aunt that it did not really matter anymore because her father was going to do to her what the black mamba and rhinoceros had failed to do.

✳ ✳ ✳

Aunt Jean was napping in the cab on the way to the hotel.

Liffey wished that she was napping too. Passing by shanty towns looking at so many people living in extreme poverty was not something that Liffey had expected to see.

She had seen street people living rough in Chicago under bridges and driven through pockets of shabby housing in Chicago but she had never before seen people living between pieces of tin and boxes and boards, although her father had told her that there were areas in the United States where people lived like that too.

When she had told Sinead she was going to a feis in South Africa, Sinead said her father went to South Africa every other year with some other Sligo people to build real houses for people who lived in these patched together scraps from dumps.

Aunt Jean was wearing a pink sleep mask so the daylight would not bother her on the ride from the airport to the hotel in Johannesburg.

✳ ✳ ✳

The city proper of Johannesburg was completely different than its outskirts. There were streets with palm trees and lovely old buildings with pillars on city blocks with parks and modern office buildings.

'There is money here,' Liffey realized. Robert Rivers told Liffey long ago that, "Where there is money, there is running water and electricity and decent housing. Where there is no money, there is squalor."

Aunt Jean was still napping when the cab stopped at the entrance to their five star hotel.

chapter 34

LIFFEY WAS POLISHING her hard shoes with the inside of a banana peel and listening to her aunt complaining.

They had been visiting museums in between practicing their Irish dance steps for the past two days. But today, Aunt Jean had worked herself up into a frenzied state of mind because it was the day before the feis.

"I do so wish that this feis was going to be held at a hotel, Liffey. I need a place to rest between stages and school halls will not have decent mirrors for my makeup retouches."

"You will do just fine, Aunt Jean. You'll be great. Don't worry about anything. I think we should check out a place called the Mai Mai Bazaar today." Liffey pointed to a brochure she had picked up in the hotel lobby.

"It will take your mind off tomorrow."

"We can shop. I want to buy some sandals there they make from old rubber tires and we can try some samosa at the Oriental Plaza."

✳ ✳ ✳

Liffey was delighted she had managed to get her aunt out of their beautiful hotel for the afternoon. The Mai Mai bazaar with its fascinating stalls could easily distract Aunt Jean all day.

There was the inyanga in her shadowy shop with thousands of dried herbs to ward off evil spirits. There were buffalo skulls, strings of colorful Zulu beads hanging everywhere, belts made of cowrie shells, snake skins and beautiful cloth.

Muti remedies for every ailment lined hundreds of shelves throughout the marketplace.

Aunt Jean was thinking about becoming a traditional African healer and wanted to learn how to concoct Muti remedies.

"It's never too late, Liffey, to broaden one's horizons. I hope you have not lost my isiZulu workbooks as I must get back to mastering the language on our flight home."

❀ ❀ ❀

The elderly Sangoma woman in the dingy shop nervously adjusted her black-string wig with hundreds of colorful beads threaded through it. Then she bent down and scooped up the yellow animal bones she had tossed on the dirt floor.

"What did you see?" Aunt Jean asked eagerly.

The woman turned and stared at Aunt Jean, then at Liffey.

'Am I imagining this or did she just take a step away from me?'

Liffey was sure the Sangoma had just deliberately distanced herself.

The Sangoma began to chant and clap her hands before she threw the bones again.

Her face looked like it had turned into a mask when she dropped to the floor on her knees and carefully examined the pattern the bones had made.

Aunt Jean looked at Liffey fearfully.

Liffey shot a frustrated 'I have no clue what is going on look' back at her aunt.

The old Sangoma woman heaved a deep sigh.

Then she shook her head back and forth sadly like she had seen something dreadful.

She stood up slowly, walked right past Aunt Jean and over to Liffey.

Her dark eyes were full of compassion and sadness when she put her hand on Liffey's shoulder and looked into her eyes.

"Girl!"

"Beware!"

"You and little brother are in shadow of serpent."

chapter 35

NEITHER LIFFEY NOR Aunt Jean felt much like eating samosa tonight. After the Sangoma lady had warned them that Liffey was in the shadow of a serpent, it was hard to relax. Even in the beautiful rooftop garden restaurant with its lovely views, it was hard to keep their spirits up. Liffey and Aunt Jean had both special ordered spaghetti and meatballs for their pre-feis good luck dinners.

"Surely, Liffey, that Sangoma woman must have meant that you have *already* been in the shadow of the serpent? The black mamba incident was only a few days ago, you know."

"No, Aunt Jean, I don't think so. She looked really sad when she told me to beware. Like something bad was going to happen to me in the future. Not like something bad had already happened."

"Well for heaven's sake, Liffey, what are the odds that you are going to see another poisonous snake here in the middle of Johannesburg? Snakes are certainly not living up here on this roof in the midst of all these beautiful flowers and shrubbery. I would say the odds are zero. That woman was confused. And you certainly do not have a little brother. It's all a lot of nonsense."

Liffey hoped her aunt was right but she had been feeling familiar warning tingles running up and down her spine ever since the little bones had formed a long, wavy line on the earthen floor.

Like a snake.

✳ ✳ ✳

"Tomorrow is your big day, Neil," Sister Helen said for the tenth time. "I will have your breakfast prepared at 6:00 a.m. The van will come for you at 7:00. When you arrive at the feis, you will go directly to your contact, a Mrs. Kibbles. She will give you your stage assignments. Make sure you ask her for anything you need. I have prepared a lunch for you in this bag along with three juice bottles."

Neil nodded politely but he was not listening anymore. How many times was Sister Helen going to go over the same information with him? She meant well but Neil was beginning to wish he had not agreed to play at this feis.

He did not want to alarm Sister Helen, but after he had another nightmare last night about a snake biting him on his legs again, little pin pricks had been running up and down his back. These neurological sensations had never happened before.

One thing was for certain, he was not sharing this information with Sister Helen. She was too busy worrying about whether or not she had forgotten to tell him something.

✳ ✳ ✳

Liffey woke up with a start. Even though Aunt Jean was probably right about the Sangoma being wrong about her being in the shadow of a serpent, Liffey decided to take extreme precautions. Her father had always told her that you can never be overly prepared for anything, especially disasters.

Aunt Jean usually created disasters so Liffey did not wake her aunt up to ask for advice.

She found the local telephone book inside a desk drawer next to her bed and looked up 'Gauteng, Johannesburg' emergency phone numbers and entered two numbers into her phone.

She retrieved her canteen with the ground up book page from Ireland and emptied it in the bathroom sink. 'This water has got to be disgusting by now with or without Saint Patrick's blessing.' She rinsed it out and refilled it with the Orange Gatorade she had purchased after the Mai Mai market. Aunt Jean had told her once that Gatorade is absorbed by the body faster than water and that was why many athletes used it to quench their thirst.

Liffey reasoned that the solid book paper particles would not float around in Gatorade as long as they would float around in water. So if she needed the blessing liquid for a snake emergency, the Gatorade would be quickly absorbed and the paper could start digesting right away in her intestines. She did not think Saint Patrick would mind. It was a small technicality. There was no Gatorade in his time.

After she had dumped a new batch of shredded book from the baggie into the canteen, she shook it up and said a quick prayer:

"Saint Patrick, pray for us."

It was 6:00 a.m. and Liffey was almost ready to go to the rooftop garden restaurant and order her pre-feis bagel with turkey, tomato slice and melted cheese. She would let Aunt Jean sleep and bring coffee and some fruit back to the room for her.

It was always impossible to predict what her aunt would want for breakfast. One day it was fruit. The next day it was toast. Then, out of nowhere, a huge stack of pancakes with a side of bacon. She knew how fragile Aunt Jean's nerves had been lately and was not going to get her aunt up this morning until it was absolutely necessary. They did not have to leave the hotel until 7:30 a.m. because the school where the feis was being held was only five miles away.

✳ ✳ ✳

The Johannesburg herper left the picnic basket containing the fourteen-foot-long Black Mamba in a white Lexis which was parked under the Toyota Motors sign in the car park. He was glad to be done with this and had no desire to learn the identity of the person he had sold his soul to.

✳ ✳ ✳

The man who had driven the white Lexis to the car park was eating a leisurely breakfast across the street in a small restaurant. From his window table, there was a clear view of the parking lot.

He watched as the Johannesburg herper drove up in a black truck and left a large picnic basket in the white Lexis.

After he finished his breakfast and his man had left in the white Lexis with the snake, he would casually cross the street, walk over to the blue Ford his man would have parked under the Toyota Motors sign, and drive it back to the rental agency.

Then he would return to his hotel in a taxi and wait for breaking news from the local media.

chapter 36

THE HANDICAPPED VAN service arrived at the Holy Infant Home for Disabled Children at 7:00 a.m. Neil had managed to escape from Sister Helen when she answered an emergency call in the infant infirmary. As the van pulled away, he realized that this was the very first time he had ever been out of the institution by himself.

Except of course for the short time he had lived with the family who had left him there.

✳ ✳ ✳

Liffey and her Aunt Jean were ready to leave for the feis when Robert Rivers called to wish them good luck.

'Maybe I am not going to be executed after all when we get back to Wisconsin,' Liffey thought optimistically. She knew that her father had every right to be furious with her and Aunt Jean. They had totally betrayed his trust by sneaking off to Africa.

Still, if Liffey *had* asked his permission, there was no doubt in her mind her father would have said, "Are you kidding?"

She hoped this sneaky expedition did not mean that her father was going to put her back in prison with Principal Godzilla.

She knew for a fact that, while it was unspoken, she had been more or less expelled from the middle school after the fire alarm event and that was fine with her.

Aunt Jean's School of Life was much more kid oriented. Liffey hoped she would be able to talk her father into continuing her studies with her aunt. At least until things got better for her mother.

Aunt Jean was now talking about taking a cruise to Alaska to observe polar bears and the midnight sun and dancing at a feis in Anchorage. Maybe her aunt would agree to let Sinead come with them.

❋ ❋ ❋

Aunt Jean was in high spirits en route to the Johannesburg Feis. "Both of us have worked hard preparing for this feis, Liffey. I am ready to face my competition and I also have a wonderful surprise for you, darling."

Liffey was not at all sure she wanted a wonderful surprise from her aunt. Aunt Jean was very eccentric and her idea of what a wonderful surprise would be could be something scary.

It was probably a new wig. 'I hope it's not floor length.'

The taxi drove down a long driveway leading to the Thomas Secondary School campus grounds. It was beautifully landscaped with red flowers lining the walks and well manicured lawns.

A large red-bricked patio with sculpted shrubbery and wooden benches was designated as the feis check in area.

"Well the time has come, Liffey. We are here representing the United States of America. It is up to us to dance our best and conduct ourselves with dignity."

"This is not the Olympics, Aunt Jean," Liffey teased. "But I agree that we should be good sports and very civilized. I won't pull anyone's wig off."

The check in table had no line. Liffey had noticed that there were only around fifty cars parked in the lot when the taxi had deposited them at the front entrance. This was surprising since it was almost 8:00 a.m. already and the dancing was to begin at 8:30. The atmosphere was very relaxed.

Two small vendor tables selling things like sock glue and poodle socks and wigs were set up in the school foyer. Liffey was very relieved that there were no sparkling stressors like crystals and rhinestones for sale that might trigger another post-traumatic bling syndrome episode from Aunt Jean.

"This is nice. It's a lot like the feis I went to in Ireland, Aunt Jean."

"Yes it is rather low key, isn't it? This might actually be a very pleasant day, Liffey. Not having to push through throngs of people from stage to stage and worry about my makeup will be a nice change."

❊ ❊ ❊

Aunt Jean looked like she was going to cry standing by the registration table, holding the envelope the registrar had handed to her.

"But I don't understand, I registered by mail because I could not find your feis website. I clearly wrote that I was an adult Irish dancer and would pay when I registered in person. I also registered my niece in Prizewinner."

"Yes, I do understand Ms. Rivers. But you forgot to put a return address on the envelope and did not give us a phone number or e-mail address to contact you so we could inform you that there are no adult dancer competitions at this feis and we could not read your signature. I myself would have contacted Irish dancing schools in Milwaukee had I been able to read your signature. But it is, as you can see, illegible and the Milwaukee postmark is all we had to go on. We had no way to contact you. You can register your niece now. I am so very, very sorry."

Liffey felt like crying for Aunt Jean. Her aunt had been dreaming of this competition for months. She had emptied their dining room of all its furniture and turned it into a dance studio so they could practice on the pinewood floor.

She pointed her toes when she drove her car. Sometimes she had practiced for eight hours a day.

The feis in New York had not gone well for Aunt Jean and she had booked the wrong walking safari because of her Post-Traumatic Bling Disorder condition.

Now this!

Liffey wondered how her aunt was going to handle this disappointment.

Aunt Jean paid Liffey's entry fees and fought back tears. She looked Liffey directly in the eye and said: "I will get through this disappointment, Liffey, darling. To tell you the truth, I am so excited about the surprise I have for you that I can actually bear this sorrow. There will be other feiseanna. Other countries. More adventures."

Liffey could not believe that Aunt Jean was taking this so well.

"Liffey, darling, come with me for the surprise of your life!"

Liffey was intrigued. She knew her aunt was a drama queen, but her excitement seemed genuine. Whatever it was she was going to give Liffey obviously meant a lot to her. Liffey could not think of anything she needed or even wanted.

'Maybe Aunt Jean has already booked a cruise to Alaska?' Liffey thought hopefully.

She followed her aunt into a remote corner of the school hall cafeteria. Aunt Jean hung her own dress carrier over a chair and placed Liffey's solo dress carrier on a long table.

✳ ✳ ✳

Neil felt very conspicuous wheeling himself around looking for the other musicians. He was not nervous about playing today because he had practiced so much that he felt like a robot.

After he checked in with Mrs. Kibbles, he found his stage and waited. It was only 7:45, but dancers were already sitting around waiting for the stage monitor to begin checking them in.

He took his violin out of its case and picked up the bow. This was official. Like Sister Helen had told him a thousand times, he was the youngest musician ever to have been chosen to play at a feis in South Africa.

It was exciting.

✳ ✳ ✳

Robert Rivers made the final arrangements with the medical transport company.

Maeve would be transferred to Knock International Airport in a few hours from Sligo. Tonight they would be home in Wisconsin. Hopefully, Liffey and Jean would turn up sometime on Sunday or Monday because Sinead would be desperate to visit with Liffey and he would be busy with Maeve.

✳ ✳ ✳

Black Mamba was starving. After days of being fed gourmet snake food, there had been nothing to eat since Thursday.

It was long past time to hunt for prey again.

chapter 37

AUNT JEAN SLOWLY unzipped Liffey's dress bag.

"Close your eyes, Liffey, darling! I'll tell you when to open them."

"What did you put in the bag with my solo dress, Aunt Jean? Maybe tickets to Alaska?"

"Open your eyes, Liffey!"

'This is not happening. This cannot be happening.' Liffey could not make her mouth, which was wide open, let any words out.

"I am not surprised that you are speechless, Liffey. It has the same effect on me too every time I look at it."

"Aunt Jean, what is this?" Liffey finally gasped, hoping against hope it was not what it appeared to be: The ugliest solo dress she had ever seen. Possibly the ugliest any kind of dress she had ever seen.

"Liffey, darling, this is your custom designed safari solo dress!"

Liffey's heart sank down to her toes. Her beautiful blue solo dress with the silver Ogham symbols was back in Wisconsin. Her aunt had switched dresses, and now expected her to be thrilled and actually dance in this monstrosity.

Liffey struggled to put a smile on her face. It was obvious that her aunt had spent considerable time and probably money on this hideous thing. 'Aunt Jean has been talking about designing Irish dance dresses, but I never imagined she would practice on me.' She tried to force another smile but large tears were running down her face.

"I can tell how overwhelmed with sheer joy you are, Liffey. Try to get a hold of yourself and I will point out the significance of the symbols."

Liffey managed to nod.

"We shall start with the cape, my dear. You will note the Buffalo Thorn Trees intricately woven together in a classic Celtic knot design."

'Actually, the tree design on the cape is pretty good, but the rest of the dress looks like a Halloween costume gone bad,' thought Liffey. The dress was a patchwork quilt made from fake animal pelts. 'For all the cave dweller Irish dancers out there,' Liffey winced. She could not believe her aunt actually expected her to wear this aberration.

"Now, we will flip the dress over and I will explain the other themes. You will note, Liffey, that the animals represented on this dress are all members of the Big Five Club."

Aunt Jean ran her fingers up and down the dress.

"You will also note the bodice of the dress is faux lion fur. Its neutral tan color offsets the sleeves which are black and white zebra striped."

"I realize I took some liberties using the zebra, which is not a Big Fiver, but I had to add some contrast."

"The chandelier skirt is trimmed with faux leopard fur and appliquéd on both sides with elephant trunks and rhinoceros horns."

For a brief moment, Liffey considered flight. In biology she had learned that there is a part of your brain that is supposed to trigger a flight instinct for survival. Like if a vampire is trying to kiss you, or Principal Godzilla's squeaky shoes were heard walking down the hall. She would tell Aunt Jean later that she had been so overcome with emotion that she had a brief nervous breakdown.

"And lastly, the grand finale solo dress crown!"

Liffey stifled a scream.

The grand finale crown was a small lion's mane which looked like it had been cut off a plush toy. It appeared to be mounted on a headband and there were tiny plastic cape buffalo horns piercing through the fake fur.

Liffey was completely panicked now. She was not going to tell her aunt that this was without question the ugliest dress, Irish dance or otherwise, that she had ever seen. Her aunt was rising above her own disappointment about not being able to adult-dance at the feis today. She would have to rise above her urge to flee from this dress.

'People will never forget me if I put this on. I will always be known as the crazy American who wore a safari themed solo dress and lion's mane crown to a feis in South Africa.'

'People will laugh when they think about me until the day they die. I will join a cloistered convent and never appear in public again.'

'On the other hand, Aunt Jean went to a lot of trouble to make this hideous thing for me and she loves it. I don't know a single person here, so after my humiliation today, I can put street clothes back on and disappear.'

"I have to be bigger than this. Aunt Jean deserves it," Liffey told herself aloud.

"Aunt Jean! I don't know how to thank you enough. This is the most creative dress I have ever seen. I love it! May I please try it on?"

Aunt Jean was thrilled that Liffey loved the dress and said, "Of course, Liffey, darling. We will do it right now."

Liffey prayed that this dress would be too small.

Or too big.

She needed a miracle.

chapter 38

THE DRESS FIT perfectly.

Liffey would have to talk to heaven later about its lack of intervention concerning this dress.

"I had better put my cover-up smock on right away, Aunt Jean, so nothing gets on this incredible dress." Aunt Jean agreed wholeheartedly. "It would be a tragedy if a careless dancer bumped into you and there was a food spill."

For now, Liffey was trying to keep a low, low profile. It was already 11:30 and she had not danced once yet. There were only two stages. She told Aunt Jean again how much she loved the dress and that she needed some fresh air. She found her backpack and left the building.

It was official. Soon Irish dancer Liffey Rivers was going to be the greatest laughing stock of all time in Irish dance history. 'I am going to be a legend.'

She found a bench out in the courtyard that was almost entirely hidden in a clump of bushes and slumped down, hoping no one would notice her there. Aunt Jean continued to be a good sport about not dancing today and seemed content to stay inside and watch the dancers.

***

Neil's stage assignment was over for the time being. It was 11:30. He had played for beginners all morning and so far, there had been only six dancers who had competed in each step.

Mrs. Kibbles told him to go and rest up because he would be playing again after lunch.

✳ ✳ ✳

Neil was hungry so he grabbed his lunch bucket and headed outside to eat in private. He hoped that Sister Helen might have put his favorite smiley face cakes in his lunch, and he did not want an audience watching him eat them.

✳ ✳ ✳

The white Lexis pulled up to the front entrance of the school. The driver was wearing an athletic cap, sunglasses, a white dress shirt and blue tie. A name tag on his shirt pocket read: Speedy Florist & Gifts. He carried a large picnic hamper and a bunch of colorful balloons that said: 'Good Luck.' He walked around in the school lobby looking for an official and was directed outside to the courtyard where the feis committee was breaking down the registration table.

"Oh how lovely!" Mrs. Esther Flanagan cooed. "Who is the lucky dancer?"

The man consulted a clipboard that he carried and said, "Liffey Rivers. I believe she is American."

"Of course. We do have a dancer from the States here today. I think I saw the American out here just a short while ago. She was walking over towards those bushes." Mrs. Flanagan pointed to the center of the courtyard.

"Thanks much," the polite delivery man answered.

He held the door open for Mrs. Flanagan and her assistants while they carried the registration table back into the school along with a box full of feis paperwork.

When he was sure they were out of sight, he walked over to the bushes and called out: "Liffey Rivers? Delivery for Liffey Rivers!"

A wigged head appeared above a shrub.

"That would be me, I guess."

"I have a gift hamper for you and these 'Good Luck' balloons."

"Looks like they were ordered from the States."

Liffey relaxed with this information.

Her wonderful father had sent her a good luck hamper!

Probably a selection of local food. Her father was always big on trying out local food whenever they traveled together.

Liffey signed the receipt and noticed that the delivery man was wearing very expensive brown leather shoes with a hole-punched design like the shoes Aunt Jean had given to her father for his birthday last year.

Robert Rivers had been outwardly polite and gracious to his sister but later told Liffey he was donating the shoes for a charity auction and that nobody on earth had the right to wear eighteen hundred dollar designer shoes.

The driver handed her the basket, nodded, and walked through the courtyard out to the front of the building.

Liffey was relieved her father was no longer angry with her. This must be a peace offering.

Little prickles started running up her arms and down her back as she tied the balloon bouquet to the bushes.

Maybe they were warning her someone was going to die from fright when they saw her safari solo dress.

chapter 39

NEIL ROBERTS LEFT the building through the front door to avoid the crowd. He would find a secluded spot in the courtyard and eat his smiley cakes before he ate the three carrots, apple and ham sandwich.

He wheeled his way through a small grove of fig trees where colorful balloons were bobbing above a row of bushes like an invitation to a birthday party.

Neil spun his chair left on to a little pathway to investigate and narrowly missed running over the feet of Liffey Rivers who was sitting on a bench next to a large picnic basket finishing up a long text to Sinead McGowan.

✳ ✳ ✳

The delivery man in the white Lexis left the school grounds, taking care not to speed and attract attention. When he had reached the end of the long driveway, he dialed the man with the lousy Afrikaans accent that he had only spoken with over the phone.

"Done," he said in English. Then he deleted the number he called and left the grounds of the Thomas Secondary School.

He removed the Speedy Florist & Gifts name tag and burned them in the car's ashtray in case he was stopped by the police. Then he headed east. After he torched the white Lexis in the abandoned warehouse garage, he would make sure the entire building was also swallowed up by the flames.

He would drive away from the unfortunate warehouse fire in the stolen black Porsche he had hidden behind the garage before the fire brigade could arrive.

✳ ✳ ✳

"Excuse me!" Neil was mortified. He was trying very hard today to blend in.

"No problem," Liffey assured him. I'm hiding out here. My name is Liffey. Want to join me?"

This was the first invitation Neil had ever received from any girl to do anything whatsoever and he quickly accepted. "Sure, that's cool." Neil sincerely hoped that this was not a pathetic thing to say.

"I just received this amazing picnic hamper and it is probably loaded with goodies. Want to help me eat them?" Neil was elated. An invitation to eat lunch with an attractive older girl!

"Sure, that's cool." This was now definitely pathetic. He had just said the same stupid thing twice in a row. Who was he trying to impress? He was not quite eleven years old and this dancer was obviously at least eighteen. She must be laughing at him big time even though she seemed very nice.

"O.K. We can check out the hamper together and when we're done feeding our faces, I'll find my Aunt Jean and share the rest with her. She usually eats like a bird so this is not as rude as it seems." Neil smiled.

"So then, let's dig in."

Liffey stood up and was unbuckling the hamper on the bench next to her when she flew back and the biggest snake Neil had ever seen exploded straight up out of the basket, swaying and hissing like one of the breathing machines in Sister Helen's infirmary.

Its hooded head was raised up at least four feet out of the basket, casting a long shadow on the ground that looked like a leafless tree branch blowing in the wind. Neil had seen one of these snakes before at the zoo and knew that it killed almost instantly. 'This American girl cannot know how bad this is.'

Liffey stood perfectly still between Black Mamba and the boy and said in an expressionless, low voice: "Get out of here now, slowly, whoever you are. Don't come any closer. This is a black mamba and I am history. A Sangoma told me this was going to happen."

Liffey was trying not to reveal how petrified she was. "Do you understand? You need to get out of here," she said again in a calm, artificial voice. "Right now. This snake is going to bite me. If I move, it will strike at once. It will bite you too if you do not back up slowly and get away from here while you can. Warn everybody and call for help."

Neil could not move. He was hypnotized by this towering serpent's beady little eyes focused on Liffey and the hollow hissing noise it made. He could not just leave this nice girl out here alone to die. Sister Helen would know what to do. She would pray or something and it would all be fine. He should have told her about the snake dreams, because he had a strong feeling that he was going to be bitten here today too, like in his dreams.

The snake lunged at Liffey and hissed.

It did not strike at her this time to bite. The zookeeper had told Neil's field trip that mambas usually lunged and stopped a few times before they attacked if they were cold. If they were not cold, they did not do test lunges and could strike faster than a bolt of fatal lightning. If you were ever confronted by a mamba, you were not supposed to move a muscle.

Liffey continued to remain perfectly still. 'Maybe she does know what to do,' Neil thought.

"Don't move sideways," Liffey said, "only straight back. Don't you move an inch either way." Or should she give him the distance not to move in metric? They used the metric system over here but Liffey could not remember now how many centimeters there were in one inch.

Liffey realized that they were both within instant striking range of this mamba, and one of them, if not both, was soon going to be attacked by this snake. It was inevitable. Its escape routes were cut off by garden walls. It had only two directions to move in—forward, right at her or past her on either side towards this poor boy who could not run.

Neil knew he had to do something. If he distracted the snake with his wheelchair, maybe Liffey would be able to escape unharmed.

How did the most feared snake in Africa get into a picnic basket here at this feis? Up until this moment, the most dangerous thing that had ever happened to him was eating Sister Loyola's lobster bisque.

'Sister Helen is not going to like this one bit,' he thought as he began to inch his wheelchair forward and to the left to get around the girl and distract the mamba, 'but this nice girl does not deserve to die today.'

Neil did not see the shadow of death coming upon him. It happened faster than the blink of an eye. The fang wounds on his legs were invisible under his trousers and because his legs had no feeling, there was no pain.

Liffey watched, petrified with fear, as the snake vanished into the bushes behind the boy after it had struck at him twice. This little boy had just saved her life at the cost of his own, and she did not even know his name! She grabbed her mobile and speed dialed the first emergency medical number she had programmed into it before she had left the hotel this morning.

When the medical dispatcher answered, Liffey spoke quickly but clearly: "A large black mamba has just bitten a young boy in a wheelchair on both of his legs. We are at the Johannesburg Feis at the Thomas Secondary School on the corner of First Street and Jasmine Avenue. We are outside in the courtyard and the snake is loose. Please hurry."

Next, Liffey dialed the police emergency number and said: "A boy has been bitten twice by a black mamba. I have already called for paramedics. There is a large black mamba loose in the courtyard of…"

Liffey tried very hard not to completely unravel. This little boy needed her help now. He was dying and she was not dying because of what he had just done for her. The poison from the mamba was already moving through his frail body.

She reached for her backpack and found the canteen filled with Saint Patrick's shredded blessing paper and Orange Gatorade. She raced over to Neil who was sitting upright in his wheelchair smiling off into the distance. "What beautiful, kind eyes he has," thought Liffey.

"Here, drink some of this fast and say a prayer to Saint Patrick," Liffey ordered, making the sign of the cross. Neil managed to get three swigs down.

She took his head into both of her hands and whispered: "You are going to be just fine. You are a hero. I owe you my life and now I am going to save yours." Liffey made sure he was not slumping forward in his wheelchair and ran into the school. She jumped up on the closest stage, past two surprised dancers who stopped cold in the middle of their hornpipes.

She signaled for the musician to stop playing and shouted over the protests of the audience who did not know what to think about a dancer they had never seen before sabotaging a competition stage.

"This is an emergency! A young boy has been bitten by a large black mamba outside in the courtyard. Do not leave this building unless you can help this boy medically or handle a mamba. I have already called emergency services."

A man ran up to Liffey from the audience past pockets of shocked parents who had already begun to collect their dancers. "Call for local help," the doctor shouted to the stage monitor. Then he turned to Liffey and said, "I'm a doctor. Let's get to that little boy."

Liffey guided him out into the courtyard where Neil sat upright in his wheelchair clutching the rosary beads that Sister Helen had tucked into his pocket. His eyelids were drooping and he was white as snow.

"I promise that everything is going to be all right. The doctor is here now." Liffey thought again that she did not even know the name of this person who had saved her life.

"Quickly," the doctor ordered. "Let's wheel him over to that patch of grass and away from these bushes. The mamba might still be in them."

"We need to lift him up carefully out of the chair and keep him as still as possible." They gently placed him on the ground and the doctor immediately removed Neil's shoes and trousers and began to examine him.

"The fang wounds are here on both thighs. They are huge and deep. This snake must be enormous. The venom from a mamba goes straight for the nerves and attacks the central nervous system. The toxins will shut down this boy's major organs in a very short time."

The doctor pointed to Liffey's canteen. "Do you have any water in your canteen?" Liffey handed it to the doctor who wet a handkerchief he took out of his pocket.

"Why is this orange?"

"It's Gatorade."

"It will do. I am going to wipe the area around the bites to get rid of any excess venom so it does not leak into the wounds. We need to work fast."

"This boy saved my life doctor."

"All right then, it's your turn to save his. Do you know CPR?"

"Yes."

"Good. We will need to be starting it soon. Right now I am going to apply pressure to the puncture wounds on both legs with my hands while you tear this shirt into long strips like ace bandages." The doctor pulled his shirt over his head and handed it to Liffey along with a Swiss Army knife. Then he pressed down on Neil's fang wounds with both hands.

Liffey sliced at the shirt and ripped it in half.

The doctor covered and wrapped the wounds tightly.

"We need to slow down the toxins moving through his system. I'm going to need another belt," he said, unbuckling his own. He quickly tied it above Neil's wound on the right leg.

Liffey ran over to her dance pack and found a scarf she tied her hair back with on hot days. "This will do fine," the doctor said. He tied the scarf tightly above Neil's left thigh wound.

"These are arterial tourniquets. We won't need to splint his legs. From the look of them, it appears that they haven't moved in a long time," he said sadly. "Poor little fellow."

The doctor listened to Neil's chest while he took his pulse. "His pulse is very faint. He's already shutting down."

"Let's start CPR now."

"I'll do the heart massage."

"Can you remove your cover-up and lay it over him? He's cold."

chapter 40

SISTER HELEN PUT the phone down slowly and held her chest with both hands. It hurt. This had to be another nightmare. Like the one she had a few nights ago. What other explanation could there be for her precious Neil lying in a courtyard unconscious after being bitten by a black mamba? She knelt down on the kitchen floor and began to pray and weep. There was nothing else she could do now until she found out where the ambulance would be taking her little angel.

✳ ✳ ✳

Mouth to mouth resuscitation was draining, and Liffey felt weak and light headed after doing it for more than five minutes until the medics finally arrived. She was happy now to see so many people working on—whoever he was. 'He saved my life and I still can't thank him by name.'

The Sangoma must have meant that he was the 'brother' who was in the shadow of the serpent with her. Except of course, he was not really her brother. 'Maybe the word for 'brother' in Zulu does not mean your actual blood brother,' Liffey thought. 'If he had not moved towards the snake, I would be the one on the respirator now with all the tubes attached.'

✳ ✳ ✳

The questions from the police started immediately: *"How big was this snake? How could she be sure it was a black mamba? What did she mean it had popped out of a picnic basket? Was there a psycho maniac at this feis? Who handed her the basket? What did he look like? Would she recognize him again if she saw him? Did she know Neil Roberts prior to this feis?"* And on and on and on…

Neil Roberts? His name is Neil Roberts? "Until today, officers, I had never seen him before in my life."

❊ ❊ ❊

The man with his right arm in a plaster cast bit the cigar he had purchased in London in half when he saw the wig girl on live television talking with reporters.

This *déjà vu* was the last straw. Was his life on automatic repeat?

Was she immortal?

Did good luck follow her around like her shadow?

What were the odds that someone she did not even know would sacrifice himself to save her life and ruin everything?

Again.

❊ ❊ ❊

The medical transport plane had taken off from Knock International Airport in County Mayo and was heading towards Canada when Robert Rivers received a text from his sister:

"Robert, just so you do not get all huffy and angry and accuse me of not keeping you informed as to your daughter's whereabouts and important, pertinent events concerning her welfare: A young boy sacrificed himself earlier today to save her life at the Johannesburg Feis when Liffey received a picnic basket containing a 14 foot Black Mamba snake, along with a dozen good luck balloons. She thought the basket was from

you. Liffey is fine. The poor boy is fighting for his life as the snake bit him twice. Liffey and I are en route to the hospital where the paramedics have taken him."

***

Steve Powers watched the news on television from the restaurant in the hotel where he and the Rivers were staying. After he had set up their taxicab ride to and from the Johannesburg Feis with a trusted friend and since nothing dangerous could possibly occur at an Irish dance competition at a secondary school in Gauteng, he had decided to spend the day relaxing around the hotel pool.

When a visibly shaken Jean Rivers appeared on the screen being interviewed by a reporter and said that her niece, who was standing in the background wearing a very peculiar animal skin dress talking with police, had opened a picnic basket which contained a large black mamba snake, he spat out his coffee, signed the check and tore out of the restaurant to the parking garage.

His tires squealed as he drove down the car park ramps, out the exit and on to the boulevard.

He had obviously messed up beyond belief and would probably be fired, but his first concern was getting the Rivers ladies out of there and then not letting them out of his sight until they boarded their South African Airways flight tomorrow back to Chicago.

He was going to blow his cover when he turned up as a detective hired by Liffey's father's office to watch over her but that was his own fault. He had let things get to this point by sheer carelessness. He did not take it seriously that a young girl like Liffey would require a private detective looking out for her every move.

Up until right now, all Liffey and her aunt had done were very normal, touristy things. He had thought her father was one of those overly-protective, rich Americans who made everything into a big drama. 'I was so wrong,' he moaned, flooring the accelerator pedal.

If whoever had sent the mamba basket to Liffey saw what he had just seen on television, he might very well be on his way there now to finish the job.

❊ ❊ ❊

Robert Rivers called his Chicago office and instructed them to get Liffey and his sister on the next plane out of Johannesburg. It did not matter where it was going in the States. "Just get them out of South Africa and back to the States immediately."

He also told his staff to arrange a police escort for his sister and daughter directly to the airport from the hospital where the boy had been taken.

He called Sam Snyder and instructed him to call Detective Powers to find out why he was not with his daughter when this whole debacle had taken place and to have Powers accompany them on their return flight to the States.

His worst fears were now confirmed. Donald Smith, a.k.a. McFleury, a.k.a. 'St. Louis Skunk Man,' was not yet history. He had not perished when his horse flipped him over the cliff on Knocknarea. He had escaped and was apparently doing business again in Africa.

Both his wife and daughter could identify this man while they were still alive.

❊ ❊ ❊

Sinead pretended to be asleep like Mrs. Rivers so Mr. Rivers could talk freely to his office.

Apparently Liffey was in the middle of some kind of catastrophe again. She really should tell Mr. Rivers that Liffey was texting her just as the picnic basket was being delivered because Liffey had described the delivery man's shoes as being identical to shoes that his sister Jean had given him for a birthday present.

Liffey had said that the delivery man's shoes were very expensive, hole-punched brown leather dress shoes. Not comfortable footwear like you would expect a delivery man to be wearing.

Sinead was too busy now thinking about the baby cuckoos and how she might be able to stop them from murdering the Irish chicks next spring. She would have to remember to tell Mr. Rivers about the shoes.

Just in case it might be important.

✳ ✳ ✳

Steve Powers arrived at the Thomas Secondary School and pushed his way through the throng of newspaper reporters and on location television crews. Liffey Rivers was not talking to reporters and was being shielded by two police officers who were doing an excellent job of keeping the media away from her.

'If looks could kill,' he thought, 'those officers would not need weapons. This place is a madhouse.'

There were at least ten people running around with snake hooks looking for the mamba. It looked as though every police officer in Gauteng was here asking questions and making the courtyard a crime scene with yellow tape and barricades.

A shout went up from the far end of the courtyard. Black Mamba was found in a drain pipe on the west side of the school and successfully transferred to a trap box. It appeared to be at least fourteen feet in length.

Before Detective Powers could reach Liffey or her aunt, a police van drove into the courtyard and they were both ushered into the vehicle over the loud protests of reporters who wanted a statement from Liffey.

He hurried back to his car and joined the parade of persistent news crew vehicles which were scrambling to get into position to follow the police van. His mobile phone rang as he turned onto Jasmine.

Attorney Rivers' office had booked him on a flight to Amsterdam with Liffey and Jean. It would continue on to Chicago. He was to leave immediately for the hotel where the Rivers' luggage would already be packed and waiting for him at the concierge desk.

The flight left at 3:30 p.m. Liffey and Jean would be driven to the Oliver Tambo Airport Security Center by the police who would wait for his arrival and transfer custody of the Rivers ladies to him.

chapter 41

THE OFFICER BEHIND the steering wheel agreed to take her passengers to the trauma center where the victim had been taken before they went to the precinct station for more questioning.

She checked her rear view mirror and was dismayed to see a long procession of cars and news trucks following them.

"Hang on ladies we're going for a ride!" Officer Pike made a fast, and unexpected, illegal U-turn. There were traffic cameras clearly in sight to warn the procession of newsmen behind them that they would get a traffic ticket and large fine if they dared to followed suit.

Officer Pike turned into a large grocery store car park and requested back up. Two minutes later, Liffey and her aunt jumped out of the van into a neighborhood squad car with darkened backseat windows.

Officer Pike sped away and the media parade picked up her trail and followed her out of the parking lot.

"She's leading them to a hospital on the other side of the city," said their new police escort driver with a smile.

"Thanks very much," Liffey said. "I don't think I can talk about this anymore until I find out how Neil Roberts is doing."

Aunt Jean agreed. "Those reporters kept asking me what you were wearing, Liffey. Can you imagine that? A poor child is fighting for his life and all they talked about was my unique safari designer dress."

Liffey winced. She had completely forgotten what she was wearing. She looked down at her leopard lap and zebra sleeves. It didn't matter anymore. She wished now she had not said a prayer that she would not have to dance in this hideous dress.

The huge trauma center where Liffey and her aunt were taken gave Liffey a surge of hope. From the outside it looked like it could handle anything inside its extensive walls. There was no sign of any reporters or television cameras as Liffey and her aunt walked quickly through the automatic doors into the reception area.

"Neil Roberts is in ICU, Unit 4. I'm afraid only family can visit with him."

Liffey heard her own voice saying: "He's my brother and this is his aunt."

"All right then. Go down the hall to the elevators. Up to the fifth floor and follow the signs."

❋ ❋ ❋

"Only one person at a time is allowed in his room," said the ICU supervisor. Aunt Jean nodded at Liffey to go ahead and sat down in the comfortable lounge.

"Visiting time is limited to five minutes every two hours. Please sanitize your hands before you go in."

Liffey braced herself and walked into a large room full of monitors and beeping sounds. In the very center of the room a pale little boy was sleeping. He was attached to three IV bags and a ventilator. "Don't let all this equipment frighten you," a young nurse said, turning off an IV drip alert alarm.

The door opened and three doctors entered. "I am afraid you will have to leave, miss. We need to evaluate this young man and adjust his antivenom therapy."

"May I please thank him for saving my life?"

"Certainly," replied the unit nurse.

Liffey walked over to the bed and clasped Neil's right hand, locking thumbs together.

The nurse repositioned Neil's breathing tube and glanced down at the intertwined hands. "Oh my! You hardly ever see two identical birth marks on siblings in the same place, especially the café-au-lait kind."

Liffey looked down and was very surprised to see that Neil and she both had the same 'coffee-with-milk' spot on their right thumbs.

Liffey tried not to reveal how thrilled she was. The old Sangoma woman had *told* her she had a little brother!

"Neil, it's your sister, Liffey Rivers," she murmured in his ear. "Thank you for saving my life. I will come back as soon as I can and we'll figure all this out together."

When Liffey unlocked her thumb from Neil's cold little hand, she noticed an almost invisible hair on the sheet. Liffey pinched it with her fingers and carefully placed it in her left hand. She knew she would not be able to bring up the biological brother theory with her father unless she had some hardcore evidence.

Then she left Unit 4 of the ICU room. If the tiny hair belonged to Neil, she would have the DNA proof she needed to bring her father back to South Africa to meet his son.

✳ ✳ ✳

Liffey left the room thinking for the thousandth time that she must live in the twilight zone where nothing is as it seems.

She walked to the lounge to get her mobile phone so she could call her father and tell him about this new turn of events. Aunt Jean was having an animated conversation with four police officers.

"Here she is officers. I told you I did not lose my niece!"

Liffey could see that Aunt Jean was very agitated. "We are being escorted to the airport Liffey by these police officers. Your father has made arrangements for us to leave the country immediately and I must say I agree with him. We cannot stay in a place where lions are sneaking around plotting to eat us."

The police officers looked taken aback but said nothing.

Liffey knew it was pointless to protest. If her father had put this leaving the country immediately thing in motion, it was going to happen no matter what she thought or said or did.

She would come back for Neil as soon as she could.

chapter 42

LIFFEY DID NOT tell her Aunt Jean that Neil Roberts was her brother. She had no evidence other than the café-au-lait birthmarks, a gut feeling, and the declaration of the Sangoma at the Mai Mai marketplace.

Leaving the hospital surrounded by four police officers made Liffey feel vulnerable and uncomfortable. She looked like a lunatic in her safari solo dress being taken off to an asylum.

But it did not matter how she felt. Neil was upstairs fighting for his life because of her.

The officers completely surrounded Liffey on the way to the police van like she was some kind of movie star being shielded from the paparazzi.

Things had moved so quickly after Neil had been bitten by the mamba that she had not had time to sort things out. Until right now, she had not thought about the fact that the snake was meant to bite her. Not poor Neil. Somebody here in South Africa wanted her dead.

She knew who it was.

✳ ✳ ✳

"Hello, ladies," a familiar voice said cheerfully from the doorway of the Oliver Tambo Airport Security Center.

"Mr. Powers! What on earth are you doing here?" Aunt Jean asked.

"Today it's Detective Steve Powers, ladies."

"Detective?" Aunt Jean was confused.

"Let me guess," said Liffey. "Attorney Robert Rivers hired you to protect me?"

"Bingo!" Steve Powers grinned.

"So now what?" Liffey was beginning to feel a wave of fear washing over her. She felt cold and clammy.

"Do you think there is going to be another attempt on my life today?"

"No. No. You don't need to think about that," Steve Powers said reassuringly. "That's why I'm here. I promise you that I am a much better detective than safari ranger! So leave the worrying to me. Here are your bags, ladies. I would imagine you might want to change into more comfortable clothing, Liffey? "

"Whatever makes you think that, Detective Powers?" Liffey laughed. He smiled and gave her a 'what-in-the-world-are-you-wearing?' look.

Aunt Jean was busy selecting her flight home wardrobe from what had to be the largest suitcase in South Africa. Liffey found jeans and her favorite green sweater and followed her aunt to the 'Employees Only' restroom.

✻ ✻ ✻

Before the South African Airways flight to Amsterdam boarded, Liffey called the hospital and was told Neil was not out of the woods yet but things looked good for him.

So far, there had been no complications and the antivenom seemed to be working.

For the first time since the snake attack, Liffey felt like she could breathe again.

Mr. Powers sat in the aisle seat. Aunt Jean took the window seat. Liffey felt safe sandwiched between them while the plane filled up with passengers stuffing their carryon luggage in the storage compartments above their seats.

✳ ✳ ✳

The plane's takeoff was uneventful and soon the captain announced that the passengers were free to move around in the cabin. Liffey yawned and asked Mr. Powers if he would mind getting her a pillow and blanket from the overhead storage bin.

"I think a nap is an excellent idea, Liffey. You must be exhausted."

Mr. Powers stood up and then leaned back in again from the aisle to allow a well dressed man in a brown leather jacket to pass by.

It was the hole-punched brown leather shoes walking down the aisle that made Liffey's heart begin to pound in her chest and the little hairs on her arms stand up on end.

She had seen those shoes before.

Earlier today.

Just before a Black Mamba snake had exploded out of a picnic basket and cast its long shadow over her and a little boy in a wheelchair.

THE END
A Brockagh Book.
www.liffeyrivers.com

Made in the USA
San Bernardino, CA
12 March 2013